Dashiell Hammett (1894–1961) was born in St Mary's County, Maryland. After spells at various menial jobs, he became an operative for Pinkerton's National Detective Agency. World War I, in which he served stateside, interrupted his sleuthing and injured his health, but his experiences as a private detective had laid the foundation for his writing career. In the late 1920s he became the unquestioned master of detective fiction in America, with work including *Red Harvest* (1929), *The Glass Key* (1930), *The Thin Man* (1934) and some eighty short stories, mostly published in *Black Mask* magazine. He died in 1961.

*By Dashiell Hammett*

NOVELS

Red Harvest
The Dain Curse
The Maltese Falcon
The Glass Key

SHORT STORIES

The Big Knockover
The Continental Op

# RED HARVEST
## DASHIELL HAMMETT

An Orion paperback

First published in the United States in 1929
This paperback edition published in 2012
by Orion Books,
an imprint of The Orion Publishing Group Ltd,
Orion House, 5 Upper St Martin's Lane,
London WC2H 9EA

An Hachette UK company

3 5 7 9 10 8 6 4

A CIP catalogue record for this book
is available from the British Library.

ISBN 978-1-4091-3808-2

Printed and bound in Great Britain
by Clays Ltd, St Ives plc

The Orion Publishing Group's policy is to use papers
that are natural, renewable and recyclable products and
made from wood grown in sustainable forests. The logging
and manufacturing processes are expected to conform to
the environmental regulations of the country of origin.

www.orionbooks.co.uk

To Joseph Thompson Shaw

# 1

# A Woman in Green
# and a Man in Gray

first heard Personville called Poisonville by a red-haired mucker named Hickey Dewey in the Big Ship in Butte. He also called his shirt a shoit. I didn't think anything of what he had done to the city's name. Later I heard men who could manage their r's give it the same pronunciation. I still didn't see anything in it but the meaningless sort of humor that used to make richardsnary the thieves' word for dictionary. A few years later I went to Personville and learned better.

Using one of the phones in the station, I called the *Herald*, asked for Donald Willsson, and told him I had arrived.

'Will you come out to my house at ten this evening?' He had a pleasantly crisp voice. 'It's 2101 Mountain Boulevard. Take a Broadway car, get off at Laurel Avenue, and walk two blocks west.'

I promised to do that. Then I rode up to the Great Western Hotel, dumped my bags, and went out to look at the city.

The city wasn't pretty. Most of its builders had gone in for gaudiness. Maybe they had been successful at first. Since then the smelters whose brick stacks stuck up tall against a gloomy mountain to the south had yellow-smoked everything into uniform dinginess. The result was an ugly city of forty thousand people, set in an ugly notch between two ugly mountains that had been all dirtied up by mining. Spread over this was a grimy sky that looked as if it had come out of the smelters' stacks.

The first policeman I saw needed a shave. The second had a couple of buttons off his shabby uniform. The third stood in the center of the city's main intersection – Broadway and Union Street – directing traffic, with a cigar in one corner of his mouth. After that I stopped checking them up.

At nine-thirty I caught a Broadway car and followed the directions Donald Willsson had given me. They brought me to a house set in a hedged grassplot on a corner.

The maid who opened the door told me Mr Willsson was not home. While I was explaining that I had an appointment with him a slender blonde woman of something less than thirty in green crêpe came to the door. When she smiled her blue eyes didn't lose their stoniness. I repeated my explanation to her.

'My husband isn't in now.' A barely noticeable accent slurred her s's. 'But if he's expecting you he'll probably be home shortly.'

She took me upstairs to a room on the Laurel Avenue side of the house, a brown and red room with a lot of books in it. We sat in leather chairs, half facing each other, half facing a burning coal grate, and she set about learning my business with her husband.

'Do you live in Personville?' she asked first.

'No. San Francisco.'

'But this isn't your first visit?'

'Yes.'

'Really? How do you like our city?'

'I haven't seen enough of it to know.' That was a lie. I had. 'I got in only this afternoon.'

Her shiny eyes stopped prying while she said:

'You'll find it a dreary place.' She returned to her digging with: 'I suppose all mining towns are like this. Are you engaged in mining?'

'Not just now.'

She looked at the clock on the mantel and said:

'It's inconsiderate of Donald to bring you out here and then keep you waiting, at this time of night, long after business hours.'

I said that was all right.

'Though perhaps it isn't a business matter,' she suggested.

I didn't say anything.

She laughed – a short laugh with something sharp in it.

'I'm really not ordinarily so much of a busybody as you probably think,' she said gaily. 'But you're so excessively secretive that I can't help being curious. You aren't a bootlegger, are you? Donald changes them so often.'

I let her get whatever she could out of a grin.

A telephone bell rang downstairs. Mrs Willsson stretched her green-slippered feet out toward the burning coal and pretended she hadn't heard the bell. I didn't know why she thought that necessary.

She began: 'I'm afraid I'll ha—' and stopped to look at the maid in the doorway.

The maid said Mrs Willsson was wanted at the phone. She excused herself and followed the maid out. She didn't go downstairs, but spoke over an extension within earshot.

I heard: 'Mrs Willsson speaking . . . Yes . . . I beg your pardon? . . . Who? . . . Can't you speak a little louder? . . . *What*? . . . Yes . . . Yes . . . Who is this? . . . Hello! Hello!'

The telephone hook rattled. Her steps sounded down the hallway – rapid steps.

I set fire to a cigarette and stared at it until I heard her going down the steps. Then I went to a window, lifted an edge of the blind, and looked out at Laurel Avenue, and at the square white garage that stood in the rear of the house on that side.

Presently a slender woman in dark coat and hat came into sight hurrying from house to garage. It was Mrs Willsson. She drove away in a Buick coupé. I went back to my chair and waited.

Three-quarters of an hour went by. At five minutes after eleven, automobile brakes screeched outside. Two minutes later Mrs Willsson came into the room. She had taken off hat and coat. Her face was white, her eyes almost black.

'I'm awfully sorry,' she said, her tight-lipped mouth moving jerkily, 'but you've had all this waiting for nothing. My husband won't be home tonight.'

I said I would get in touch with him at the *Herald* in the morning.

I went away wondering why the green toe of her left slipper was dark and damp with something that could have been blood.

I walked over to Broadway and caught a street car. Three blocks north of my hotel I got off to see what the crowd was doing around a side entrance of the City Hall.

Thirty or forty men and a sprinkling of women stood on the sidewalk looking at a door marked *Police Department*. There were men from mines and smelters still in their working clothes, gaudy boys from pool rooms and dance halls, sleek men with slick pale faces, men with the dull look of respectable husbands, a few just as respectable and dull women, and some ladies of the night.

On the edge of this congregation I stopped beside a square-set man in rumpled gray clothes. His face was grayish too, even the thick lips, though he wasn't much older than thirty. His face was broad, thick-featured and intelligent. For color he depended on a red windsor tie that blossomed over his gray flannel shirt.

'What's the rumpus?' I asked him.

He looked at me carefully before he replied, as if he wanted to be sure that the information was going into safe hands. His eyes were gray as his clothes, but not so soft.

'Don Willsson's gone to sit on the right hand of God, if God don't mind looking at bullet holes.'

'Who shot him?' I asked.

The gray man scratched the back of his neck and said:

'Somebody with a gun.'

I wanted information, not wit. I would have tried my luck with some other member of the crowd if the red tie hadn't interested me. I said:

'I'm a stranger in town. Hang the Punch and Judy on me. That's what strangers are for.'

'Donald Willsson, Esquire, publisher of the *Morning* and *Evening Heralds*, was found in Hurricane Street a little while ago, shot very dead by parties unknown,' he recited in a rapid sing-song. 'Does that keep your feelings from being hurt?'

'Thanks.' I put out a finger and touched a loose end of his tie. 'Mean anything? Or just wearing it?'

'I'm Bill Quint.'

'The hell you are!' I exclaimed, trying to place the name. 'By God, I'm glad to meet you!'

I dug out my card case and ran through the collection of credentials I had picked up here and there by one means or another. The red card was the one I wanted. It identified me as Henry F. Neill, A. B. seaman, member in good standing of the Industrial Workers of the World. There wasn't a word of truth in it.

I passed this card to Bill Quint. He read it carefully, front and back, returned it to my hand, and looked me over from hat to shoes, not trustfully.

'He's not going to die any more,' he said. 'Which way you going?'

'Any.'

We walked down the street together, turned a corner, aimlessly as far as I knew.

'What brought you in here, if you're a sailor?' he asked casually.

'Where'd you get that idea?'

'There's the card.'

'I got another that proves I'm a timber beast,' I said. 'If you want me to be a miner I'll get one for that tomorrow.'

'You won't. I run 'em here.'

'Suppose you got a wire from Chi?' I asked.

'Hell with Chi! I run 'em here.' He nodded at a restaurant door and asked: 'Drink?'

'Only when I can get it.'

We went through the restaurant, up a flight of steps, and into a narrow second-story room with a long bar and a row of tables. Bill Quint nodded and said, 'Hullo!' to some of the boys and girls at tables and bar, and steered me into one of the green-curtained booths that lined the wall opposite the bar.

We spent the next two hours drinking whiskey and talking.

The gray man didn't think I had any right to the card I had showed him, nor to the other one I had mentioned. He didn't think I was a good wobbly. As chief muckademuck of the I. W. W. in Personville, he considered it his duty to get the low-down on me, and to not let himself be pumped about radical affairs while he was doing it.

That was all right with me. I was interested in Personville affairs. He didn't mind discussing them between casual pokings into my business with the red cards.

What I got out of him amounted to this:

For forty years old Elihu Willsson – father of the man who had been killed this night – had owned Personville, heart, soul, skin and guts. He was president and majority stockholder of the Personville Mining Corporation, ditto of the First National Bank, owner of the *Morning Herald*, and *Evening Herald*, the city's only newspapers, and at least part owner of nearly every other enterprise of any importance. Along with these pieces of property he owned a United States senator, a couple of representatives, the governor, the mayor, and most of the state legislature. Elihu Willsson was Personville, and he was almost the whole state.

Back in the war days the I. W. W. – in full bloom then throughout the West – had lined up the Personville Mining Corporation's help. The help hadn't been exactly pampered.

They used their new strength to demand the things they wanted. Old Elihu gave them what he had to give them, and bided his time.

In 1921 it came. Business was rotten. Old Elihu didn't care whether he shut down for a while or not. He tore up the agreements he had made with his men and began kicking them back into their pre-war circumstances.

Of course the help yelled for help. Bill Quint was sent out from I. W. W. headquarters in Chicago to give them some action. He was against a strike, an open walk-out. He advised the old sabotage racket, staying on the job and gumming things up from the inside. But that wasn't active enough for the Personville crew. They wanted to put themselves on the map, make labor history.

They struck.

The strike lasted eight months. Both sides bled plenty. The wobblies had to do their own bleeding. Old Elihu hired gunmen, strike-breakers, national guardsmen and even parts of the regular army, to do his. When the last skull had been cracked, the last rib kicked in, organized labor in Personville was a used fire-cracker.

But, said Bill Quint, old Elihu didn't know his Italian history. He won the strike, but he lost his hold on the city and the state. To beat the miners he had to let his hired thugs run wild. When the fight was over he couldn't get rid of them. He had given his city to them and he wasn't strong enough to take it away from them. Personville looked good to them and they took it over. They had won his strike for him and they took the city for their spoils. He couldn't openly break with them. They had too much on him. He was responsible for all they had done during the strike.

Bill Quint and I were both fairly mellow by the time we had got this far. He emptied his glass again, pushed his hair out of his eyes and brought his history up to date:

'The strongest of 'em now is probably Pete the Finn. This

stuff we're drinking's his. Then there's Lew Yard. He's got a
loan shop down on Parker Street, does a lot of bail bond
business, handles most of the burg's hot stuff, so they tell me,
and is pretty thick with Noonan, the chief of police. This kid
Max Thaler – Whisper – has got a lot of friends too. A little
slick dark guy with something wrong with his throat. Can't talk.
Gambler. Those three, with Noonan, just about help Elihu run
his city – help him more than he wants. But he's got to play
with 'em or else—'

'This fellow who was knocked off tonight – Elihu's son –
where did he stand?' I asked.

'Where papa put him, and he's where papa put him now.'

'You mean the old man had him—?'

'Maybe, but that's not my guess. This Don just came home
and began running the papers for the old man. It wasn't like the
old devil, even if he was getting close to the grave, to let
anybody cop anything from him without hitting back. But he
had to be cagey with these guys. He brought the boy and his
French wife home from Paris and used him for his monkey – a
damned nice fatherly trick. Don starts a reform campaign in the
papers. Clear the burg of vice and corruption – which means
clear it of Pete and Lew and Whisper, if it goes far enough. Get
it? The old man's using the boy to shake 'em loose. I guess they
got tired of being shook.'

'There seems to be a few things wrong with that guess,' I said.

'There's more than a few things wrong with everything in this
lousy burg. Had enough of this paint?'

I said I had. We went down to the street. Bill Quint told me
he was living in the Miners' Hotel in Forest Street. His way
home ran past my hotel, so we walked down together. In front
of my hotel a beefy fellow with the look of a plain-clothes man
stood on the curb and talked to the occupant of a Stutz touring
car.

'That's Whisper in the car,' Bill Quint told me.

I looked past the beefy man and saw Thaler's profile. It was young, dark and small, with pretty features as regular as if they had been cut by a die.

'He's cute,' I said.

'Uh-huh,' the gray man agreed, 'and so's dynamite.'

# 2
# The Czar of
# Poisonville

The *Morning Herald* gave two pages to Donald Willsson and his death. His picture showed a pleasant intelligent face with curly hair, smiling eyes and mouth, a cleft chin and a striped necktie.

The story of his death was simple. At ten-forty the previous night he had been shot four times in stomach, chest and back, dying immediately. The shooting had taken place in the eleven-hundred block of Hurricane Street. Residents of that block who looked out after hearing the shots saw the dead man lying on the sidewalk. A man and a woman were bending over him. The street was too dark for anyone to see anybody or anything clearly. The man and woman had disappeared before anybody else reached the street. Nobody knew what they looked like. Nobody had seen them go away.

Six shots had been fired at Willsson from a .32 caliber pistol. Two of them had missed him, going into the front wall of a house. Tracing the course of these two bullets, the police had learned that the shooting had been done from a narrow alley across the street. That was all anybody knew.

Editorially the *Morning Herald* gave a summary of the dead man's short career as a civic reformer and expressed a belief that he had been killed by some of the people who didn't want Personville cleaned up. The *Herald* said the chief of police could best show his own lack of complicity by speedily catching and convicting the murderer or murderers. The editorial was blunt and bitter.

I finished it with my second cup of coffee, jumped a Broadway car, dropped off at Laurel Avenue, and turned down toward the dead man's house.

I was half a block from it when something changed my mind and my destination.

A smallish young man in three shades of brown crossed the street ahead of me. His dark profile was pretty. He was Max Thaler, alias Whisper. I reached the corner of Mountain Boulevard in time to catch the flash of his brown-covered rear leg vanishing into the late Donald Willsson's doorway.

I went back to Broadway, found a drug store with a phone booth in it, searched the directory for Elihu Willsson's residence number, called it, told somebody who claimed to be the old man's secretary that I had been brought from San Francisco by Donald Willsson, that I knew something about his death, and that I wanted to see his father.

When I made it emphatic enough I got an invitation to call.

The czar of Poisonville was propped up in bed when his secretary – a noiseless slim sharp-eyed man of forty – brought me into the bedroom.

The old man's head was small and almost perfectly round under its close-cut crop of white hair. His ears were too small and plastered too flat to the sides of his head to spoil the spherical effect. His nose also was small, carrying down the curve of his bony forehead. Mouth and chin were straight lines chopping the sphere off. Below them a short thick neck ran down into white pajamas between square meaty shoulders. One of his arms was outside the covers, a short compact arm that ended in a thick-fingered blunt hand. His eyes were round, blue, small and watery. They looked as if they were hiding behind the watery film and under the bushy white brows only until the time came to jump out and grab something. He wasn't the sort of man whose pocket you'd try to pick unless you had a lot of confidence in your fingers.

He ordered me into a bedside chair with a two-inch jerk of his round head, chased the secretary away with another, and asked:

'What's this about my son?'

His voice was harsh. His chest had too much and his mouth too little to do with his words for them to be very clear.

'I'm a Continental Detective Agency operative, San Francisco branch,' I told him. 'A couple of days ago we got a check from your son and a letter asking that a man be sent here to do some work for him. I'm the man. He told me to come out to his house last night. I did, but he didn't show up. When I got downtown I learned he had been killed.'

Elihu Willsson peered suspiciously at me and asked:

'Well, what of it?'

'While I was waiting your daughter-in-law got a phone message, went out, came back with what looked like blood on her shoe, and told me her husband wouldn't be home. He was shot at ten-forty. She went out at ten-twenty, came back at eleven-five.'

The old man sat straight up in bed and called young Mrs Willsson a flock of things. When he ran out of words of that sort he still had some breath left. He used it to shout at me:

'Is she in jail?'

I said I didn't think so.

He didn't like her not being in jail. He was nasty about it. He bawled a lot of things I didn't like, winding up with:

'What the hell are you waiting for?'

He was too old and too sick to be smacked. I laughed and said:

'For evidence.'

'Evidence? What do you need? You've—'

'Don't be a chump,' I interrupted his bawling. 'Why should she kill him?'

'Because she's a French hussy! Because she—'

The secretary's frightened face appeared at the door.

'Get out of here!' the old man roared at it, and the face went.

'She jealous?' I asked before he could go on with his shouting. 'And if you don't yell maybe I'll be able to hear you anyway. My deafness is a lot better since I've been eating yeast.'

He put a fist on top of each hump his thighs made in the covers and pushed his square chin at me.

'Old as I am and sick as I am,' he said very deliberately, 'I've a great mind to get up and kick your behind.'

I paid no attention to that, repeating:

'Was she jealous?'

'She was,' he said, not yelling now, 'and domineering, and spoiled, and suspicious, and greedy, and mean, and unscrupulous, and deceitful, and selfish, and damned bad – altogether damned bad!'

'Any reason for her jealousy?'

'I hope so,' he said bitterly. 'I'd hate to think a son of mine would be faithful to her. Though likely enough he was. He'd do things like that.'

'But you don't know any reason why she should have killed him?'

'Don't know any reason?' He was bellowing again. 'Haven't I been telling you that—'

'Yeah. But none of that means anything. It's kind of childish.'

The old man flung the covers back from his legs and started to get out of bed. Then he thought better of it, raised his red face and roared:

'Stanley!'

The door opened to let the secretary glide in.

'Throw this bastard out!' his master ordered, waving a fist at me.

The secretary turned to me. I shook my head and suggested: 'Better get help.'

He frowned. We were about the same age. He was weedy, nearly a head taller than I, but fifty pounds lighter. Some of my hundred and ninety pounds were fat, but not all of them. The secretary fidgeted, smiled apologetically, and went away.

'What I was about to say,' I told the old man: 'I intended talking to your son's wife this morning. But I saw Max Thaler go into the house, so I postponed my visit.'

Elihu Willsson carefully pulled the covers up over his legs again, leaned his head back on the pillows, screwed his eyes up at the ceiling, and said:

'Hm-m-m, so that's the way it is, is it?'

'Mean anything?'

'She killed him,' he said certainly. 'That's what it means.'

Feet made noises in the hall, huskier feet than the secretary's. When they were just outside the door I began a sentence:

'You were using your son to run a—'

'Get out of here!' the old man yelled at those in the doorway. 'And keep that door closed.' He glowered at me and demanded: 'What was I using my son for?'

'To put the knife in Thaler, Yard and the Finn.'

'You're a liar.'

'I didn't invent the story. It's all over Personville.'

'It's a lie. I gave him the papers. He did what he wanted with them.'

'You ought to explain that to your playmates. They'd believe you.'

'What they believe be damned! What I'm telling you is so.'

'What of it? Your son won't come back to life just because he was killed by mistake – if he was.'

'That woman killed him.'

'Maybe.'

'Damn you and your maybes! She did.'

'Maybe. But the other angle has got to be looked into too – the political end. You can tell me—'

'I can tell you that that French hussy killed him, and I can tell you that any other damned numbskull notions you've got are way off the lode.'

'But they've got to be looked into,' I insisted. 'And you know the inside of Personville politics better than anyone else I'm likely to find. He was your son. The least you can do is—'

'The least I can do,' he bellowed, 'is tell you to get to hell back to Frisco, you and your numbskull—'

I got up and said unpleasantly:

'I'm at the Great Western Hotel. Don't bother me unless you want to talk sense for a change.'

I went out of the bedroom and down the stairs. The secretary hovered around the bottom step, smiling apologetically.

'A fine old rowdy,' I growled.

'A remarkably vital personality,' he murmured.

At the office of the *Herald*, I hunted up the murdered man's secretary. She was a small girl of nineteen or twenty with wide chestnut eyes, light brown hair and a pale pretty face. Her name was Lewis.

She said she hadn't known anything about my being called to Personville by her employer.

'But then,' she explained, 'Mr Willsson always liked to keep everything to himself as long as he could. It was – I don't think he trusted anybody here, completely.'

'Not you?'

She flushed and said:

'No. But of course he had been here such a short while and didn't know any of us very well.'

'There must have been more to it than that.'

'Well,' she bit her lip and made a row of forefinger prints down the polished edge of the dead man's desk, 'his father wasn't – wasn't in sympathy with what he was doing. Since his father really owned the papers, I suppose it was natural for Mr Donald to think some of the employees might be more loyal to Mr Elihu than to him.'

'The old man wasn't in favor of the reform campaign? Why did he stand for it, if the papers were his?'

She bent her head to study the finger prints she had made. Her voice was low.

'It's not easy to understand unless you know— The last time Mr Elihu was taken sick he sent for Donald – Mr Donald. Mr Donald had lived in Europe most of his life, you know. Dr Pride told Mr Elihu that he'd have to give up the management of his affairs, so he cabled his son to come home. But when Mr Donald got here Mr Elihu couldn't make up his mind to let go of everything. But he wanted Mr Donald to stay here, so he gave him the newspapers – that is, made him publisher. Mr Donald liked that. He had been interested in journalism in Paris. When he found out how terrible everything was here – in civic affairs and so on – he started that reform campaign. He didn't know – he had been away since he was a boy – he didn't know—'

'He didn't know his father was in it as deep as anybody else,' I helped her along.

She squirmed a little over her examination of the finger prints, didn't contradict me, and went on:

'Mr Elihu and he had a quarrel. Mr Elihu told him to stop stirring things up, but he wouldn't stop. Maybe he would have stopped if he had known – all there was to know. But I don't suppose it would have occurred to him that his father was really seriously implicated. And his father wouldn't tell him. I suppose it would be hard for a father to tell a son a thing like that. He threatened to take the papers away from Mr Donald. I don't know whether he intended to or not. But he was taken sick again, and everything went along as it did.'

'Donald Willsson didn't confide in you?' I asked.

'No.' It was almost a whisper.

'Then, you learned all this where?'

'I'm trying – trying to help you learn who murdered him,' she said earnestly. 'You've no right to—'

'You'll help me most just now by telling me where you learned all this,' I insisted.

She stared at the desk, chewing her lower lip. I waited. Presently she said:

'My father is Mr Willsson's secretary.'

'Thanks.'

'But you mustn't think that we—'

'It's nothing to me,' I assured her. 'What was Willsson doing in Hurricane Street last night when he had a date with me at his house?'

She said she didn't know. I asked her if she had heard him tell me, over the phone, to come to his house at ten o'clock. She said she had.

'What did he do after that? Try to remember every least thing that was said and done from then until you left at the end of the day.'

She leaned back in her chair, shut her eyes and wrinkled her forehead.

'You called up – if it was you he told to come to his house – at about two o'clock. After that Mr Donald dictated some letters, one to a paper mill, one to Senator Keefer about some changes in post office regulations, and— Oh, yes! He went out for about twenty minutes, a little before three. And before he went he wrote out a check.'

'Who for?'

'I don't know, but I saw him writing it.'

'Where's his check book? Carry it with him?'

'It's here.' She jumped up, went around to the front of his desk, and tried the top drawer. 'Locked.'

I joined her, straightened out a wire clip, and with that and a blade of my knife fiddled the drawer open.

The girl took out a thin, flat First National Bank check book. The last used stub was marked $5,000. Nothing else. No name. No explanation.

'He went out with this check,' I said, 'and was gone twenty minutes? Long enough to get to the bank and back?'

'It wouldn't have taken him more than five minutes to get there.'

'Didn't anything else happen before he wrote out the check? Think. Any messages? Letters? Phone calls?'

'Let's see.' She shut her eyes again. 'He was dictating some mail and— Oh, how stupid of me! He did have a phone call. He said: "Yes, I can be there at ten, but I shall have to hurry away." Then again he said: "Very well, at ten." That was all he said except, "Yes, yes," several times.'

'Talking to a man or a woman?'

'I didn't know.'

'Think. There'd be a difference in his voice.'

She thought and said:

'Then it was a woman.'

'Which of you – you or he – left first in the evening?'

'I did. He – I told you my father is Mr Elihu's secretary. He and Mr Donald had an engagement for the early part of the evening – something about the paper's finances. Father came in a little after five. They were going to dinner together, I think.'

That was all the Lewis girl could give me. She knew nothing that would explain Willsson's presence in the eleven-hundred block of Hurricane Street, she said. She admitted knowing nothing about Mrs Willsson.

We frisked the dead man's desk, and dug up nothing in any way informative. I went up against the girls at the switchboard, and learned nothing. I put in an hour's work on messengers, city editors, and the like, and my pumping brought up nothing. The dead man, as his secretary said, had been a good hand at keeping his affairs to himself.

# 3
# Dinah Brand

At the First National Bank I got hold of an assistant cashier named Albury, a nice-looking blond youngster of twenty-five or so.

'I certified the check for Willsson,' he said after I had explained what I was up to. 'It was drawn to the order of Dinah Brand – $5,000.'

'Know who she is?'

'Oh, yes! I know her.'

'Mind telling me what you know about her?'

'Not at all. I'd be glad to, but I'm already eight minutes overdue at a meeting with—'

'Can you have dinner with me this evening and give it to me then?'

'That'll be fine,' he said.

'Seven o'clock at the Great Western?'

'Righto.'

'I'll run along and let you get to your meeting, but tell me, has she an account here?'

'Yes, and she deposited the check this morning. The police have it.'

'Yeah? And where does she live?'

'1232 Hurricane Street.'

I said: 'Well, well!' and, 'See you tonight,' and went away.

My next stop was in the office of the chief of police, in the City Hall.

Noonan, the chief, was a fat man with twinkling greenish eyes set in a round jovial face. When I told him what I was doing in his city he seemed glad of it. He gave me a hand-shake, a cigar and a chair.

'Now,' he said when we were settled, 'tell me who turned the trick.'

'The secret's safe with me.'

'You and me both,' he said cheerfully through smoke. 'But what do you guess?'

'I'm not good at guessing, especially when I haven't got the facts.'

' 'Twon't take long to give you all the facts there is,' he said. 'Willsson got a five-grand check in Dinah Brand's name certified yesterday just before bank closing. Last night he was killed by slugs from a .32 less than a block from her house. People that heard the shooting saw a man and a woman bending over the remains. Bright and early this morning the said Dinah Brand deposits the said check in the said bank. Well?'

'Who is this Dinah Brand?'

The chief dumped the ash off his cigar in the center of his desk, flourished the cigar in his fat hand, and said:

'A soiled dove, as the fellow says, a de luxe hustler, a big-league gold-digger.'

'Gone up against her yet?'

'No. There's a couple of slants to be taken care of first. We're keeping an eye on her and waiting. This I've told you is under the hat.'

'Yeah. Now listen to this,' and I told him what I had seen and heard while waiting in Donald Willsson's house the previous night.

When I had finished the chief bunched his fat mouth, whistled softly, and exclaimed:

'Man, that's an interesting thing you've been telling me! So it was blood on her slipper? And she said her husband wouldn't be home?'

'That's what I took it for,' I said to the first question, and, 'Yeah,' to the second.

'Have you done any talking to her since then?' he asked.

'No. I was up that way this morning, but a young fellow named Thaler went into the house ahead of me, so I put off my visit.'

'Grease us twice!' His greenish eyes glittered happily. 'Are you telling me the Whisper was there?'

'Yeah.'

He threw his cigar on the floor, stood up, planted his fat hands on the desk top, and leaned over them toward me, oozing delight from every pore.

'Man, you've done something,' he purred. 'Dinah Brand is this Whisper's woman. Let's me and you just go out and kind of talk to the widow.'

We climbed out of the chief's car in front of Mrs Willsson's residence. The chief stopped for a second with one foot on the bottom step to look at the black crêpe hanging over the bell. Then he said, 'Well, what's got to be done has got to be done,' and we went up the steps.

Mrs Willsson wasn't anxious to see us, but people usually see the chief of police if he insists. This one did. We were taken upstairs to where Donald Willsson's widow sat in the library. She was in black. Her blue eyes had frost in them.

Noonan and I took turns mumbling condolences and then he began:

'We just wanted to ask you a couple of questions. For instance, like where'd you go last night?'

She looked disagreeably at me, then back to the chief, frowned, and spoke haughtily:

'May I ask why I am being questioned in this manner?'

I wondered how many times I had heard that question, word for word and tone for tone, while the chief, disregarding it, went on amiably:

'And then there was something about one of your shoes being stained. The right one, or maybe the left. Anyways it was one or the other.'

A muscle began twitching in her upper lip.

'Was that all?' the chief asked me. Before I could answer he made a clucking noise with his tongue and turned his genial face to the woman again. 'I almost forgot. There was a matter of how you knew your husband wouldn't be home.'

She got up, unsteadily, holding the back of her chair with one white hand.

'I'm sure you'll excuse—'

' 'S all right.' The chief made a big-hearted gesture with one beefy paw. 'We don't want to bother you. Just where you went, and about the shoe, and how you knew he wasn't coming back. And, come to think of it, there's another— What Thaler wanted here this morning.'

Mrs Willsson sat down again, very rigidly. The chief looked at her. A smile that tried to be tender made funny lines and humps in his fat face. After a little while her shoulders began to relax, her chin went lower, a curve came in her back.

I put a chair facing her and sat on it.

'You'll have to tell us, Mrs Willsson,' I said, making it as sympathetic as I could. 'These things have got to be explained.'

'Do you think I have anything to hide?' she asked defiantly, sitting up straight and stiff again, turning each word out very precisely, except that the s's were a bit slurred. 'I did go out. The stain was blood. I knew my husband was dead. Thaler came to see me about my husband's death. Are your questions answered now?'

'We knew all that,' I said. 'We're asking you to explain them.'

She stood up again, said angrily:

'I dislike your manner. I refuse to submit to—'

Noonan said:

'That's perfectly all right, Mrs Willsson, only we'll have to ask you to go down to the Hall with us.'

She turned her back to him, took a deep breath and threw words at me:

'While we were waiting here for Donald I had a telephone call. It was a man who wouldn't give his name. He said Donald had gone to the home of a woman named Dinah Brand with a check for five thousand dollars. He gave me her address. Then I drove out there and waited down the street in the car until Donald came out.

'While I was waiting there I saw Max Thaler, whom I knew by sight. He went to the woman's house, but didn't go in. He went away. Then Donald came out and walked down the street. He didn't see me. I didn't want him to. I intended to drive home – get here before he came. I had just started the engine when I heard the shots, and I saw Donald fall. I got out of the car and ran over to him. He was dead. I was frantic. Then Thaler came. He said if I were found there they would say I had killed him. He made me run back to the car and drive home.'

Tears were in her eyes. Through the water her eyes studied my face, apparently trying to learn how I took the story. I didn't say anything. She asked:

'Is that what you wanted?'

'Practically,' Noonan said. He had walked around to one side. 'What did Thaler say this afternoon?'

'He urged me to keep quiet.' Her voice had become small and flat. 'He said either or both of us would be suspected if anyone learned we were there, because Donald had been killed coming from the woman's house after giving her money.'

'Where did the shots come from?' the chief asked.

24

'I don't know. I didn't see anything – except – when I looked up – Donald falling.'

'Did Thaler fire them?'

'No,' she said quickly. Then her mouth and eyes spread. She put a hand to her breast. 'I don't know. I didn't think so, and he said he didn't. I don't know where he was. I don't know why I never thought he might have.'

'What do you think now?' Noonan asked.

'He – he may have.'

The chief winked at me, an athletic wink in which all his facial muscles took part, and cast a little farther back:

'And you don't know who called you up?'

'He wouldn't tell me his name.'

'Didn't recognize his voice?'

'No.'

'What kind of voice was it?'

'He talked in an undertone, as if afraid of being overheard. I had difficulty understanding him.'

'He whispered?' The chief's mouth hung open as the last sound left it. His greenish eyes sparkled greedily between their pads of fat.

'Yes, a hoarse whisper.'

The chief shut his mouth with a click, opened it again to say persuasively:

'You've heard Thaler talk . . .'

The woman started and stared big-eyed from the chief to me.

'It was he,' she cried. 'It was he.'

Robert Albury, the young assistant cashier of the First National Bank, was sitting in the lobby when I returned to the Great Western Hotel. We went up to my room, had some ice-water brought, used its ice to put chill in Scotch, lemon juice, and grenadine, and then went down to the dining room.

'Now tell me about the lady,' I said when we were working on the soup.

'Have you seen her yet?' he asked.

'Not yet.'

'But you've heard something about her?'

'Only that's she's an expert in her line.'

'She is,' he agreed. 'I suppose you'll see her. You'll be disappointed at first. Then, without being able to say how or when it happened, you'll find you've forgotten your disappointment, and the first thing you know you'll be telling her your life's history, and all your troubles and hopes.' He laughed with boyish shyness. 'And then you're caught, absolutely caught.'

'Thanks for the warning. How'd you come by the information?'

He grinned shamefacedly across his suspended soup spoon and confessed:

'I bought it.'

'Then I suppose it cost you plenty. I hear she likes *dinero*.'

'She's money-mad, all right, but somehow you don't mind it. She's so thoroughly mercenary, so frankly greedy, that there's nothing disagreeable about it. You'll understand what I mean when you know her.'

'Maybe. Mind telling me how you happened to part with her?'

'No, I don't mind. I spent it all, that's how.'

'Cold-blooded like that?'

His face flushed a little. He nodded.

'You seem to have taken it well,' I said.

'There was nothing else to do.' The flush in his pleasant young face deepened and he spoke hesitantly. 'It happens I owe her something for it. She – I'm going to tell you this. I want you to see this side of her. I had a little money. After that was gone— You must remember I was young and head over heels. After my money was gone there was the bank's. I had— You don't care whether I had actually done anything or was simply thinking about it. Anyway, she found it out. I never could hide anything from her. And that was the end.'

'She broke off with you?'

'Yes, thank God! If it hadn't been for her you might be looking for me now – for embezzlement. I owe her that!' He wrinkled his forehead earnestly. 'You won't say anything about this – you know what I mean. But I wanted you to know she has her good side too. You'll hear enough about the other.'

'Maybe she has. Or maybe it was just that she didn't think she'd get enough to pay for the risk of being caught in a jam.'

He turned this over in his mind and then shook his head.

'That may have had something to do with it, but not all.'

'I gathered she was strictly pay-as-you-enter.'

'How about Dan Rolff?' he asked.

'Who's he?'

'He's supposed to be her brother, or half-brother, or something of the sort. He isn't. He's a down-and-outer – t. b. He lives with her. She keeps him. She's not in love with him or anything. She simply found him somewhere and took him in.'

'Any more?'

'There was that radical chap she used to run around with. It's not likely she got much money out of him.'

'What radical chap?'

'He came here during the strike – Quint is his name.'

'So he was on her list?'

'That's supposed to be the reason he stayed here after the strike was over.'

'So he's still on her list?'

'No. She told me she was afraid of him. He had threatened to kill her.'

'She seems to have had everybody on her string at one time or another,' I said.

'Everybody she wanted,' he said, and he said it seriously.

'Donald Willsson was the latest?' I asked.

'I don't know,' he said. 'I had never heard anything about them, had never seen anything. The chief of police had us try to find any checks he may have issued to her before yesterday, but we found nothing. Nobody could remember ever having seen any.'

'Who was her last customer, so far as you know?'

'Lately I've seen her around town quite often with a chap named Thaler – he runs a couple of gambling houses here. They call him Whisper. You've probably heard of him.'

At eight-thirty I left young Albury and set out for the Miners' Hotel in Forest Street. Half a block from the hotel I met Bill Quint.

'Hello!' I hailed him. 'I was on my way down to see you.'

He stopped in front of me, looked me up and down, growled:

'So you're a gum-shoe.'

'That's the bunk,' I complained. 'I come all the way down here to rope you, and you're smarted up.'

'What do you want to know now?' he asked.

'About Donald Willsson. You knew him, didn't you?'

'I knew him.'

'Very well?'

'No.'

'What did you think of him?'

He pursed his gray lips, by forcing breath between them made a noise like a rag tearing, and said:

'A lousy liberal.'

'You know Dinah Brand?' I asked.

'I know her.' His neck was shorter and thicker than it had been.

'Think she killed Willsson?'

'Sure. It's a kick in the pants.'

'Then you didn't?'

'Hell, yes,' he said, 'the pair of us together. Got any more questions?'

'Yeah, but I'll save my breath. You'd only lie to me.'

I walked back to Broadway, found a taxi, and told the driver to take me to 1232 Hurricane Street.

# 4
# Hurricane Street

My destination was a gray frame cottage. When I rang the bell the door was opened by a thin man with a tired face that had no color in it except a red spot the size of a half-dollar high on each cheek. This, I thought, is the lunger Dan Rolff.

'I'd like to see Miss Brand,' I told him.

'What name shall I tell her?' His voice was a sick man's and an educated man's.

'It wouldn't mean anything to her. I want to see her about Willsson's death.'

He looked at me with level tired dark eyes and said:

'Yes?'

'I'm from the San Francisco office of the Continental Detective Agency. We're interested in the murder.'

'That's nice of you,' he said ironically. 'Come in.'

I went in, into a ground-floor room where a young woman sat at a table that had a lot of papers on it. Some of the papers were financial service bulletins, stock and bond market forecasts. One was a racing chart.

The room was disorderly, cluttered up. There were too many

pieces of furniture in it, and none of them seemed to be in its proper place.

'Dinah,' the lunger introduced me, 'this gentleman has come from San Francisco on behalf of the Continental Detective Agency to inquire into Mr Donald Willsson's demise.'

The young woman got up, kicked a couple of newspapers out of her way, and came to me with one hand out.

She was an inch or two taller than I, which made her about five feet eight. She had a broad-shouldered, full-breasted, round-hipped body and big muscular legs. The hand she gave me was soft, warm, strong. Her face was the face of a girl of twenty-five already showing signs of wear. Little lines crossed the corners of her big ripe mouth. Fainter lines were beginning to make nets around her thick-lashed eyes. They were large eyes, blue and a bit blood-shot.

Her coarse hair – brown – needed trimming and was parted crookedly. One side of her upper lip had been rouged higher than the other. Her dress was of a particularly unbecoming wine color, and it gaped here and there down one side, where she had neglected to snap the fasteners or they had popped open. There was a run down the front of her left stocking.

This was the Dinah Brand who took her pick of Poisonville's men, according to what I had been told.

'His father sent for you, of course,' she said while she moved a pair of lizard-skin slippers and a cup and saucer off a chair to make room for me.

Her voice was soft, lazy.

I told her the truth:

'Donald Willsson sent for me. I was waiting to see him while he was being killed.'

'Don't go away, Dan,' she called to Rolff.

He came back into the room. She returned to her place at the table. He sat on the opposite side, leaning his thin face on a thin hand, looking at me without interest.

She drew her brows together, making two creases between them, and asked:

'You mean he knew someone meant to kill him?'

'I don't know. He didn't say what he wanted. Maybe just help in the reform campaign.'

'But do you—'

I made a complaint:

'It's no fun being a sleuth when somebody steals your stuff, does all the questioning.'

'I like to find out what's going on,' she said, a little laugh gurgling down in her throat.

'I'm that way too. For instance, I'd like to know why you made him have the check certified.'

Very casually, Dan Rolff shifted in his chair, leaning back, lowering his thin hands out of sight below the table's edge.

'So you found out about that?' Dinah Brand asked. She crossed left leg over right and looked down. Her eyes focused on the run in her stocking. 'Honest to God, I'm going to stop wearing them!' she complained. 'I'm going barefooted. I paid five bucks for these socks yesterday. Now look at the damned things. Every day – runs, runs, runs!'

'It's no secret,' I said. 'I mean the check, not the runs. Noonan's got it.'

She looked at Rolff, who stopped watching me long enough to nod once.

'If you talked my language,' she drawled, looking narrow-eyed at me, 'I might be able to give you some help.'

'Maybe if I knew what it was.'

'Money,' she explained, 'the more the better. I like it.'

I became proverbial:

'Money saved is money earned. I can save you money and grief.'

'That doesn't mean anything to me,' she said, 'though it sounds like it's meant to.'

'The police haven't asked you anything about the check?'

She shook her head, no.

I said:

'Noonan's figuring on hanging the rap on you as well as on Whisper.'

'Don't scare me,' she lisped. 'I'm only a child.'

'Noonan knows that Thaler knew about the check. He knows that Thaler came here while Willsson was here, but didn't get in. He knows that Thaler was hanging around the neighborhood when Willsson was shot. He knows that Thaler and a woman were seen bending over the dead man.'

The girl picked up a pencil from the table and thoughtfully scratched her cheek with it. The pencil made little curly black lines over the rouge.

Rolff's eyes had lost their weariness. They were bright, feverish, fixed on mine. He leaned forward, but kept his hands out of sight below the table.

'Those things,' he said, 'concern Thaler, not Miss Brand.'

'Thaler and Miss Brand aren't strangers,' I said. 'Willsson brought a five-thousand-dollar check here, and was killed leaving. That way, Miss Brand might have had trouble cashing it – if Willsson hadn't been thoughtful enough to get it certified.'

'My God!' the girl protested, 'if I'd been going to kill him I'd have done it in here where nobody could have seen it, or waited until he got out of sight of the house. What kind of a dumb onion do you take me for?'

'I'm not sure you killed him,' I said. 'I'm just sure that the fat chief means to hang it on you.'

'What are you trying to do?' she asked.

'Learn who killed him. Not who could have or might have, but who did.'

'I could give you some help,' she said, 'but there'd have to be something in it for me.'

'Safety,' I reminded her, but she shook her head.

'I mean it would have to get me something in a financial way.

It'd be worth something to you, and you ought to pay something, even if not a fortune.'

'Can't be done.' I grinned at her. 'Forget the bank roll and go in for charity. Pretend I'm Bill Quint.'

Dan Rolff started up from his chair, lips white as the rest of his face. He sat down again when the girl laughed – a lazy, good-natured laugh.

'He thinks I didn't make any profit out of Bill, Dan.' She leaned over and put a hand on my knee. 'Suppose you knew far enough ahead that a company's employees were going to strike, and when, and then far enough ahead when they were going to call the strike off. Could you take that info and some capital to the stock market and do yourself some good playing with the company's stock? You bet you could!' she wound up triumphantly. 'So you don't go around thinking that Bill didn't pay his way.'

'You've been spoiled,' I said.

'What in the name of God's the use of being so tight?' she demanded. 'It's not like it had to come out of your pocket. You've got an expense account, haven't you?'

I didn't say anything. She frowned at me, at the run in her stocking, and at Rolff. Then she said to him:

'Maybe he'd loosen up if he had a drink.'

The thin man got up and went out of the room.

She pouted at me, prodded my skin with her toe, and said:

'It's not so much the money. It's the principle of the thing. If a girl's got something that's worth something to somebody, she's a boob if she doesn't collect.'

I grinned.

'Why don't you be a good guy?' she begged.

Dan Rolff came in with a siphon, a bottle of gin, some lemons, and a bowl of cracked ice. We had a drink apiece. The lunger went away. The girl and I wrangled over the money question while we had more drinks. I kept trying to keep the conversation on Thaler and Willsson. She kept switching it to the money she deserved. It went on that way until the gin bottle was empty. My watch said one-fifteen.

She chewed a piece of lemon peel and said for the thirtieth or fortieth time:

'It won't come out of your pocket. What do you care?'

'It's not the money,' I said, 'it's the principle of the thing.'

She made a face at me and put her glass where she thought the table was. She was eight inches wrong. I don't remember if the glass broke when it hit the floor, or what happened to it. I do remember that I was encouraged by her missing the table.

'Another thing,' I opened up a new argumentative line, 'I'm not sure I really need whatever you can tell me. If I have to get along without it, I think I can.'

'It'll be nice if you can, but don't forget I'm the last person who saw him alive, except whoever killed him.'

'Wrong,' I said. 'His wife saw him come out, walk away, and fall.'

'His wife!'

'Yeah. She was sitting in a coupé down the street.'

'How did she know he was here?'

'She says Thaler phoned her that her husband had come here with the check.'

'You're trying to kid me,' the girl said. 'Max couldn't have known it.'

'I'm telling you what Mrs Willsson told Noonan and me.'

The girl spit what was left of the lemon peel out on the floor, further disarranged her hair by running her fingers through it, wiped her mouth with the back of her hand, and slapped the table.

'All right, Mr Knowitall,' she said, 'I'm going to play with you. You can think it's not going to cost you anything, but I'll get mine before we're through. You think I won't?' she challenged me, peering at me as if I were a block away.

This was no time to revive the money argument, so I said: 'I hope you do.' I think I said it three or four times, quite earnestly.

'I will. Now listen to me. You're drunk, and I'm drunk, and I'm just exactly drunk enough to tell you anything you want to know. That's the kind of girl I am. If I like a person I'll tell them anything they want to know. Just ask me. Go ahead, ask me.'

I did:

'What did Willsson give you five thousand dollars for?'

'For fun.' She leaned back to laugh. Then: 'Listen. He was hunting for scandal. I had some of it, some affidavits and things that I thought might be good for a piece of change some day. I'm a girl that likes to pick up a little jack when she can. So I had put these things away. When Donald began going after scalps I let him know that I had these things, and that they were for sale. I gave him enough of a peep at them to let him know they were good. And they were good. Then we talked about how much. He wasn't as tight as you – nobody ever was – but he was a little bit close. So the bargain hung fire, till yesterday.

'Then I gave him the rush, phoned him and told him I had another customer for the stuff and that if he wanted it he'd have to show up that night with either five thousand smacks in cash or a certified check. That was hooey, but he hadn't been around much, so he fell for it.'

'Why ten o'clock?' I asked.

'Why not? That's as good a time as any other. The main thing on a deal like that is to give them a definite time. Now you want to know why it had to be cash or a certified check? All right, I'll tell you. I'll tell you anything you want to know. That's the kind of girl I am. Always was.'

She went on that way for five minutes, telling me in detail just which and what sort of a girl she was, and always had been, and why. I yes-yes'd her until I got a chance to cut in with:

'All right, now why did it have to be a certified check?'

She shut one eye, waggled a forefinger at me, and said:

'So he couldn't stop payment. Because he couldn't have used

the stuff I sold him. It was good, all right. It was too good. It would have put his old man in jail with the rest of them. It would have nailed Papa Elihu tighter than anyone else.'

I laughed with her while I tried to keep my head above the gin I had guzzled.

'Who else would it nail?' I asked.

'The whole damned lot of them.' She waved a hand. 'Max, Lew Yard, Pete, Noonan, and Elihu Willsson – the whole damned lot of them.'

'Did Max Thaler know what you were doing?'

'Of course not – nobody but Donald Willsson.'

'Sure of that?'

'Sure I'm sure. You don't think I was going around bragging about it ahead of time, do you?'

'Who do you think knows about it now?'

'I don't care,' she said. 'It was only a joke on him. He couldn't have used the stuff.'

'Do you think the birds whose secrets you sold will see anything funny in it? Noonan's trying to hang the killing on you and Thaler. That means he found the stuff in Donald Willsson's pocket. They all thought old Elihu was using his son to break them, didn't they?'

'Yes, sir,' she said, 'and I'm one who thinks the same thing.'

'You're probably wrong, but that doesn't matter. If Noonan found the things you sold Donald Willsson in his pocket, and learned you had sold them to him, why shouldn't he add that up to mean that you and your friend Thaler had gone over to old Elihu's side?'

'He can see that old Elihu would be hurt as much as anybody else.'

'What was this junk you sold him?'

'They built a new City Hall three years ago,' she said, 'and none of them lost any money on it. If Noonan got the papers he'll pretty soon find out that they tied as much on old Elihu, or more, than on anybody else.'

'That doesn't make any difference. He'll take it for granted that the old man had found an out for himself. Take my word for it, sister, Noonan and his friends think you and Thaler and Elihu are double-crossing them.'

'I don't give a damn what they think,' she said obstinately. 'It was only a joke. That's all I meant it for. That's all it was.'

'That's good,' I growled. 'You can go to the gallows with a clear conscience. Have you seen Thaler since the murder?'

'No, but Max didn't kill him, if that's what you think, even if he was around.'

'Why?'

'Lots of reasons. First place, Max wouldn't have done it himself. He'd have had somebody else do it, and he'd have been way off with an alibi nobody could shake. Second place, Max carried a .38, and anybody he sent to do the job would have had that much gun or more. What kind of a gunman would use a .32?'

'Then who did it?'

'I've told you all I know,' she said. 'I've told you too much.'

I stood up and said:

'No, you've told me just exactly enough.'

'You mean you think you know who killed him?'

'Yeah, though there's a couple of things I'll have to cover before I make the pinch.'

'Who? Who?' She stood up, suddenly almost sober, tugging at my lapels. 'Tell me who did it.'

'Not now.'

'Be a good guy.'

'Not now.'

She let go my lapels, put her hands behind her, and laughed in my face.

'All right. Keep it to yourself – and try to figure out which part of what I told you is the truth.'

I said:

'Thanks for the part that is, anyhow, and for the gin. And if Max Thaler means anything to you, you ought to pass him the word that Noonan's trying to rib him.'

# 5
# Old Elihu Talks Sense

It was close to two-thirty in the morning when I reached the hotel. With my key the night clerk gave me a memorandum that asked me to call Poplar 605. I knew the number. It was Elihu Willsson's.

'When did this come?' I asked the clerk.

'A little after one.'

That sounded urgent. I went back to a booth and put in the call. The old man's secretary answered, asking me to come out at once. I promised to hurry, asked the clerk to get me a taxi, and went up to my room for a shot of Scotch.

I would rather have been cold sober, but I wasn't. If the night held more work for me I didn't want to go to it with alcohol dying in me. The snifter revived me a lot. I poured more of the King George into a flask, pocketed it, and went down to the taxi.

Elihu Willsson's house was lighted from top to bottom. The secretary opened the front door before I could get my finger on the button. His thin body was shivering in pale blue pajamas and dark blue bathrobe. His thin face was full of excitement.

'Hurry!' he said. 'Mr Willsson is waiting. And, please, will you try to persuade him to let us have the body removed?'

I promised and followed him up to the old man's bedroom.

Old Elihu was in bed as before, but now a black automatic pistol lay on the covers close to one of his pink hands.

As soon as I appeared he took his head off the pillows, sat upright and barked at me:

'Have you got as much guts as you've got gall?'

His face was an unhealthy dark red. The film was gone from his eyes. They were hard and hot.

I let his question wait while I looked at the corpse on the floor between door and bed.

A short thick-set man in brown lay on his back with dead eyes staring at the ceiling from under the visor of a gray cap. A piece of his jaw had been knocked off. His chin was tilted to show where another bullet had gone through tie and collar to make a hole in his neck. One arm was bent under him. The other hand held a blackjack as big as a milk bottle. There was a lot of blood.

I looked up from this mess to the old man. His grin was vicious and idiotic.

'You're a great talker,' he said. 'I know that. A two-fisted, you-be-damned man with your words. But have you got anything else? Have you got the guts to match your gall? Or is it just the language you've got?'

There was no use in trying to get along with the old boy. I scowled and reminded him:

'Didn't I tell you not to bother me unless you wanted to talk sense for a change?'

'You did, my lad.' There was a foolish sort of triumph in his voice. 'And I'll talk you your sense. I want a man to clean this pig-sty of a Poisonville for me, to smoke out the rats, little and big. It's a man's job. Are you a man?'

'What's the use of getting poetic about it?' I growled. 'If you've got a fairly honest piece of work to be done in my line, and you want to pay a decent price, maybe I'll take it on. But a lot of foolishness about smoking rats and pig-pens doesn't mean anything to me.'

'All right. I want Personville emptied of its crooks and grafters. Is that plain enough language for you?'

'You didn't want it this morning,' I said. 'Why do you want it now?'

The explanation was profane and lengthy and given to me in a loud and blustering voice. The substance of it was that he had built Personville brick by brick with his own hands and he was going to keep it or wipe it off the side of the hill. Nobody could threaten him in his own city, no matter who they were. He had let them alone, but when they started telling him, Elihu Willsson, what he had to do and what he couldn't do, he would show them who was who. He brought the speech to an end by pointing at the corpse and boasting:

'That'll show them there's still a sting in the old man.'

I wished I were sober. His clowning puzzled me. I couldn't put my finger on the something behind it.

'Your playmates sent him?' I asked, nodding at the dead man.

'I only talked to him with this,' he said, patting the automatic on the bed, 'but I reckon they did.'

'How did it happen?'

'It happened simple enough. I heard the door opening, and I switched on the light, and there he was, and I shot him, and there he is.'

'What time?'

'It was about one o'clock.'

'And you've let him lie there all this time?'

'That I have.' The old man laughed savagely and began blustering again: 'Does the sight of a dead man turn your stomach? Or is it his spirit you're afraid of?'

I laughed at him. Now I had it. The old boy was scared stiff. Fright was the something behind his clowning. That was why he blustered, and why he wouldn't let them take the body away. He wanted it there to look at, to keep panic away, visible proof of his ability to defend himself. I knew where I stood.

'You really want the town cleaned up?' I asked.

'I said I did and I do.'

'I'd have to have a free hand – no favors to anybody – run the job as I pleased. And I'd have to have a ten-thousand-dollar retainer.'

'Ten thousand dollars! Why in hell should I give that much to a man I don't know from Adam? A man who's done nothing I know of but talk?'

'Be serious. When I say *me*, I mean the Continental. You know them.'

'I do. And they know me. And they ought to know I'm good for—'

'That's not the idea. These people you want taken to the cleaners were friends of yours yesterday. Maybe they will be friends again next week. I don't care about that. But I'm not playing politics for you. I'm not hiring out to help you kick them back in line – with the job being called off then. If you want the job done you'll plank down enough money to pay for a complete job. Any that's left over will be returned to you. But you're going to get a complete job or nothing. That's the way it'll have to be. Take it or leave it.'

'I'll damned well leave it,' he bawled.

He let me get half-way down the stairs before he called me back.

'I'm an old man,' he grumbled. 'If I was ten years younger—' He glared at me and worked his lips together. 'I'll give you your damned check.'

'And authority to go through with it in my own way?'

'Yes.'

'We'll get it done now. Where's your secretary?'

Willsson pushed a button on his bedside table and the silent secretary appeared from wherever he had been hiding. I told him:

'Mr Willsson wants to issue a ten-thousand-dollar check to the Continental Detective Agency, and he wants to write the Agency – San Francisco branch – a letter authorizing the

Agency to use the ten thousand dollars investigating crime and political corruption in Personville. The letter is to state clearly that the Agency is to conduct the investigation as it sees fit.'

The secretary looked questioningly at the old man, who frowned and ducked his round white head.

'But first,' I told the secretary as he glided toward the door, 'you'd better phone the police that we've got a dead burglar here. Then call Mr Willsson's doctor.'

The old man declared he didn't want any damned doctors.

'You're going to have a nice shot in the arm so you can sleep,' I promised him, stepping over the corpse to take the black gun from the bed. 'I'm going to stay here tonight and we'll spend most of tomorrow sifting Poisonville affairs.'

The old man was tired. His voice, when he profanely and somewhat long-windedly told me what he thought of my impudence in deciding what was best for him, barely shook the windows.

I took off the dead man's cap for a better look at his face. It didn't mean anything to me. I put the cap back in place.

When I straightened up the old man asked, moderately:

'Are you getting anywhere in your hunt for Donald's murderer?'

'I think so. Another day ought to see it finished.'

'Who?' he asked.

The secretary came in with the letter and the check. I gave them to the old man instead of an answer to his question. He put a shaky signature on each, and I had them folded in my pocket when the police arrived.

The first copper into the room was the chief himself, fat Noonan. He nodded amiably at Willsson, shook hands with me, and looked with twinkling greenish eyes at the dead man.

'Well, well,' he said. 'It's a good job he did, whoever did it. Yakima Shorty. And will you look at the sap he's toting?' He kicked the blackjack out of the dead man's hand. 'Big enough to sink a battleship. You drop him?' he asked me.

'Mr Willsson.'

'Well, that certainly is fine,' he congratulated the old man. 'You saved a lot of people a lot of troubles, including me. Pack him out, boys,' he said to the four men behind him.

The two in uniform picked Yakima Shorty up by legs and arm-pits and went away with him, while one of the others gathered up the blackjack and a flashlight that had been under the body.

'If everybody did that to their prowlers, it would certainly be fine,' the chief babbled on. He brought three cigars out of a pocket, threw one over on the bed, stuck one at me, and put the other in his mouth. 'I was just wondering where I could get hold of you,' he told me as we lighted up. 'I got a little job ahead that I thought you'd like to be in on. That's how I happened to be on tap when the rumble came.' He put his mouth close to my ear and whispered: 'Going to pick up Whisper. Want to go along?'

'Yeah.'

'I thought you would. Hello, Doc!'

He shook hands with a man who had just come in, a little plump man with a tired oval face and gray eyes that still had sleep in them.

The doctor went to the bed, where one of Noonan's men was asking Willsson about the shooting. I followed the secretary into the hall and asked him:

'Any men in the house besides you?'

'Yes, the chauffeur, the Chinese cook.'

'Let the chauffeur stay in the old man's room tonight. I'm going out with Noonan. I'll get back as soon as I can. I don't think there'll be any more excitement here, but no matter what happens don't leave the old man alone. And don't leave him alone with Noonan or any of Noonan's crew.'

The secretary's mouth and eyes popped wide.

'What time did you leave Donald Willsson last night?' I asked.

'You mean night before last, the night he was killed?'

'Yeah.'

'At precisely half-past nine.'

'You were with him from five o'clock till then?'

'From a quarter after five. We went over some statements and that sort of thing in his office until nearly eight o'clock. Then we went to Bayard's and finished our business over our dinners. He left at half-past nine, saying he had an engagement.'

'What else did he say about this engagement?'

'Nothing else.'

'Didn't give you any hint of where he was going, who he was going to meet?'

'He merely said he had an engagement.'

'And you didn't know anything about it?'

'No. Why? Did you think I did?'

'I thought he might have said something.' I switched back to tonight's doings: 'What visitors did Willsson have today, not counting the one he shot?'

'You'll have to pardon me,' the secretary said, smiling apologetically, 'I can't tell you that without Mr Willsson's permission. I'm sorry.'

'Weren't some of the local powers here? Say Lew Yard, or—'

The secretary shook his head, repeating:

'I'm sorry.'

'We won't fight over it,' I said giving it up and starting back toward the bedroom door.

The doctor came out, buttoning his overcoat.

'He will sleep now,' he said hurriedly. 'Someone should stay with him. I shall be in in the morning.' He ran downstairs.

I went into the bedroom. The chief and the man who had questioned Willsson were standing by the bed. The chief grinned as if he were glad to see me. The other man scowled. Willsson was lying on his back, staring at the ceiling.

'That's about all there is here,' Noonan said. 'What say we mosey along?'

I agreed and said, 'Good-night,' to the old man. He said, 'Good-night,' without looking at me. The secretary came in with the chauffeur, a tall sunburned young husky.

The chief, the other sleuth – a police lieutenant named McGraw – and I went downstairs and got into the chief's car. McGraw sat beside the driver. The chief and I sat in back.

'We'll make the pinch along about daylight,' Noonan explained as we rode. 'Whisper's got a joint over on King Street. He generally leaves there along about daylight. We could crash the place, but that'd mean gun-play, and it's just as well to take it easy. We'll pick him up when he leaves.'

I wondered if he meant pick him up or pick him off. I asked:

'Got enough on him to make the rap stick?'

'Enough?' He laughed good-naturedly. 'If what the Willsson dame give us ain't enough to stretch him I'm a pickpocket.'

I thought of a couple of wisecrack answers to that. I kept them to myself.

# 6

# Whisper's Joint

Our ride ended under a line of trees in a dark street not far from the center of town. We got out of the car and walked down to the corner.

A burly man in a gray overcoat, with a gray hat pulled down over his eyes, came to meet us.

'Whisper's hep,' the burly man told the chief. 'He phoned Donohoe that he's going to stay in his joint. If you think you can pull him out, try it, he says.'

Noonan chuckled, scratched an ear, and asked pleasantly:

'How many would you say was in there with him?'

'Fifty, anyhow.'

'Aw, now! There wouldn't be that many, not at this time of morning.'

'The hell there wouldn't,' the burly man snarled. 'They been drifting in since midnight.'

'Is that so? A leak somewheres. Maybe you oughtn't to have let them in.'

'Maybe I oughtn't.' The burly man was angry. 'But I did what you told me. You said let anybody go in or out that wanted to, but when Whisper showed to—'

'To pinch him,' the chief said.

'Well, yes,' the burly man agreed, looking savagely at me.

More men joined us and we held a talk-fest. Everybody was in a bad humor except the chief. He seemed to enjoy it all. I didn't know why.

Whisper's joint was a three-story brick building in the middle of the block, between two two-story buildings. The ground floor of his joint was occupied by a cigar store that served as entrance and cover for the gambling establishment upstairs. Inside, if the burly man's information was to be depended on, Whisper had collected half a hundred friends, loaded for a fight. Outside, Noonan's force was spread around the building, in the street in front, in the alley in back, and on the adjoining roofs.

'Well, boys,' the chief said amiably after everybody had had his say, 'I don't reckon Whisper wants trouble any more than we do, or he'd have tried to shoot his way out before this, if he's got that many with him, though I don't mind saying I don't think he has – not that many.'

The burly man said: 'The hell he ain't.'

'So if he don't want trouble,' Noonan went on, 'maybe talking might do some good. You run over, Nick, and see if you can't argue him into being peaceable.'

The burly man said: 'The hell I will.'

'Phone him, then,' the chief suggested.

The burly man growled: 'That's more like it,' and went away.

When he came back he looked completely satisfied.

'He says,' he reported, ' "Go to hell." '

'Get the rest of the boys down here,' Noonan said cheerfully. 'We'll knock it over as soon as it gets light.'

The burly Nick and I went around with the chief while he made sure his men were properly placed. I didn't think much of them – a shabby, shifty-eyed crew without enthusiasm for the job ahead of them.

The sky became a faded gray. The chief, Nick, and I stopped in a plumber's doorway diagonally across the street from our target.

Whisper's joint was dark, the upper windows blank, blinds down over cigar store windows and door.

'I hate to start this without giving Whisper a chance,' Noonan said. 'He's not a bad kid. But there's no use me trying to talk to him. He never did like me much.'

He looked at me. I said nothing.

'You wouldn't want to make a stab at it?' he asked.

'Yeah, I'll try it.'

'That's fine of you. I'll certainly appreciate it if you will. You just see if you can talk him into coming along without any fuss. You know what to say – for his own good and all that, like it is.'

'Yeah,' I said and walked across to the cigar store, taking pains to let my hands be seen swinging empty at my sides.

Day was still a little way off. The street was the color of smoke. My feet made a lot of noise on the pavement.

I stopped in front of the door and knocked the glass with a knuckle, not heavily. The green blind down inside the door made a mirror of the glass. In it I saw two men moving up the other side of the street.

No sound came from inside. I knocked harder, then slid my hand down to rattle the knob.

Advice came from indoors:

'Get away from there while you're able.'

It was a muffled voice, but not a whisper, so probably not Whisper's.

'I want to talk to Thaler,' I said.

'Go talk to the lard-can that sent you.'

'I'm not talking for Noonan. Is Thaler where he can hear me?'

A pause. Then the muffled voice said: 'Yes.'

'I'm the Continental op who tipped Dinah Brand off that Noonan was framing you,' I said. 'I want five minutes' talk with you. I've got nothing to do with Noonan except to queer his racket. I'm alone. I'll drop my rod in the street if you say so. Let me in.'

I waited. It depended on whether the girl had got to him with the story of my interview with her. I waited what seemed a long time.

The muffled voice said:

'When we open, come in quick. And no stunts.'

'All set.'

The latch clicked. I plunged in with the door.

Across the street a dozen guns emptied themselves. Glass shot from door and windows tinkled around us.

Somebody tripped me. Fear gave me three brains and half a dozen eyes. I was in a tough spot. Noonan had slipped me a pretty dose. These birds couldn't help thinking I was playing his game.

I tumbled down, twisting around to face the door. My gun was in my hand by the time I hit the floor.

Across the street, burly Nick had stepped out of a doorway to pump slugs at us with both hands.

I steadied my gun-arm on the floor. Nick's body showed over the front sight. I squeezed the gun. Nick stopped shooting. He crossed his guns on his chest and went down in a pile on the sidewalk.

Hands on my ankles dragged me back. The floor scraped pieces off my chin. The door slammed shut. Some comedian said:

'Uh-huh, people don't like you.'

I sat up and shouted through the racket:

'I wasn't in on this.'

The shooting dwindled, stopped. Door and window blinds were dotted with gray holes. A husky whisper said in the darkness:

'Tod, you and Slats keep an eye on things down here. The rest of us might as well go upstairs.'

We went through a room behind the store, into a passageway, up a flight of carpeted steps, and into a second-story room that held a green table banked for crap-shooting. It was a small room, had no windows, and the lights were on.

There were five of us. Thaler sat down and lit a cigarette, a small dark young man with a face that was pretty in a chorus-man way until you took another look at the thin hard mouth. An angular blond kid of no more than twenty in tweeds sprawled on his back on a couch and blew cigarette smoke at the ceiling. Another boy, as blond and as young, but not so angular, was busy straightening his scarlet tie, smoothing his yellow hair. A thin-faced man of thirty with little or no chin under a wide loose mouth wandered up and down the room looking bored and humming *Rosy Cheeks*.

I sat in a chair two or three feet from Thaler's.

'How long is Noonan going to keep this up?' he asked. There was no emotion in his hoarse whispering voice, only a shade of annoyance.

'He's after you this trip,' I said. 'I think he's going through with it.'

The gambler smiled a thin, contemptuous smile.

'He ought to know what a swell chance he's got of hanging a one-legged rap like that on me.'

'He's not figuring on proving anything in court,' I said.

'No?'

'You're to be knocked off resisting arrest, or trying to make a get-away. He won't need much of a case after that.'

'He's getting tough in his old age.' The thin lips curved in another smile. He didn't seem to think much of the fat chief's deadliness. 'Any time he rubs me out I deserve rubbing. What's he got against you?'

'He's guessed I'm going to make a nuisance of myself.'

'Too bad. Dinah told me you were a pretty good guy, except kind of Scotch with the roll.'

'I had a nice visit. Will you tell me what you know about Donald Willsson's killing?'

'His wife plugged him.'

'You saw her?'

'I saw her the next second – with the gat in her hand.'

'That's no good to either of us,' I said. 'I don't know how far you've got it cooked. Rigged right, you could make it stick in court, maybe, but you'll not get a chance to make your play there. If Noonan takes you at all he'll take you stiff. Give me the straight of it. I only need that to pop the job.'

He dropped his cigarette on the floor, mashed it under his foot, and asked:

'You that hot?'

'Give me your slant on it and I'm ready to make the pinch – if I can get out of here.'

He lit another cigarette and asked:

'Mrs Willsson said it was me that phoned her?'

'Yeah – after Noonan had persuaded her. She believes it now – maybe.'

'You dropped Big Nick,' he said. 'I'll take a chance on you. A man phoned me that night. I don't know him, don't know who he was. He said Willsson had gone to Dinah's with a check for five grand. What the hell did I care? But, see, it was funny somebody I didn't know cracked it to me. So I went around. Dan stalled me away from the door. That was all right. But still it was funny as hell that guy phoned me.

'I went up the street and took a plant in a vestibule. I saw Mrs Willsson's heap standing in the street, but I didn't know then that it was hers or that she was in it. He came out pretty soon and walked down the street. I didn't see the shots. I heard them. Then this woman jumps out of the heap and runs over to him. I knew she hadn't done the shooting. I ought to have beat it. But it was all funny as hell, so when I saw the woman was Willsson's wife I went over to them, trying to find out what it was all about. That was a break, see? So I had to make an out for myself, in case something slipped. I strung the woman. That's the whole damned works – on the level.'

'Thanks,' I said. 'That's what I came for. Now the trick is to get out of here without being mowed down.'

'No trick at all,' Thaler assured me. 'We go any time we want to.'

'I want to now. If I were you, I'd go too. You've got Noonan pegged as a false-alarm, but why take a chance? Make the sneak and keep under cover till noon, and his frame-up will be a wash-out.'

Thaler put his hand in his pants pocket and brought out a fat roll of paper money. He counted off a hundred or two, some fifties, twenties, tens, and held them out to the chinless man, saying:

'Buy us a get-away, Jerry, and you don't have to give anybody any more dough than he's used to.'

Jerry took the money, picked up a hat from the table, and strolled out. Half an hour later he returned and gave some of the bills back to Thaler, saying casually:

'We wait in the kitchen till we get the office.'

We went down to the kitchen. It was dark there. More men joined us.

Jerry opened the door and we went down three steps into the back yard. It was almost full daylight. There were ten of us in the party.

'This all?' I asked Thaler.

He nodded.

'Nick said there were fifty of you.'

'Fifty of us to stand off that crummy force!' he sneered.

A uniformed copper held the back gate open, muttering nervously:

'Hurry it up, boys, please.'

I was willing to hurry, but nobody else paid any attention to him.

We crossed an alley, were beckoned through another gate by a big man in brown, passed through a house, out into the next street, and climbed into a black automobile that stood at the curb.

One of the blond boys drove. He knew what speed was.

I said I wanted to be dropped off somewhere in the neighbor-hood of the Great Western Hotel. The driver looked at

Whisper, who nodded. Five minutes later I got out in front of my hotel.

'See you later,' the gambler whispered, and the car slid away.

The last I saw of it was its police department license plate vanishing around a corner.

# 7
# That's Why
# I Sewed You Up

It was half-past five. I walked around a few blocks until I came to an unlighted electric sign that said *Hotel Crawford*, climbed a flight of steps to the second-floor office, registered, left a call for ten o'clock, was shown into a shabby room, moved some of the Scotch from my flask to my stomach, and took old Elihu's ten-thousand-dollar check and my gun to bed with me.

At ten I dressed, went up to the First National Bank, found young Albury, and asked him to certify Willsson's check for me. He kept me waiting a while. I suppose he phoned the old man's residence to find out if the check was on the up-and-up. Finally he brought it back to me, properly scribbled on.

I sponged an envelope, put the old man's letter and check in it, addressed it to the Agency in San Francisco, stuck a stamp on it, and went out and dropped it in the mail-box on the corner.

Then I returned to the bank and said to the boy:

'Now tell me why you killed him.'

He smiled and asked:

'Cock Robin or President Lincoln?'

'You're not going to admit off-hand that you killed Donald Willsson?'

'I don't want to be disagreeable,' he said, still smiling, 'but I'd rather not.'

'That's going to make it bad,' I complained. 'We can't stand here and argue very long without being interrupted. Who's the stout party with cheaters coming this way?'

The boy's face pinkened. He said:

'Mr Dritton, the cashier.'

'Introduce me.'

The boy looked uncomfortable, but he called the cashier's name. Dritton – a large man with a smooth pink face, a fringe of white hair around an otherwise bald pink head, and rimless nose glasses – came over to us.

The assistant cashier mumbled the introductions. I shook Dritton's hand without losing sight of the boy.

'I was just saying,' I addressed Dritton, 'that we ought to have a more private place to talk in. He probably won't confess till I've worked on him a while, and I don't want everybody in the bank to hear me yelling at him.'

'Confess?' The cashier's tongue showed between his lips.

'Sure.' I kept my face, voice and manner bland, mimicking Noonan. 'Didn't you know that Albury is the fellow who killed Donald Willsson?'

A polite smile at what he thought an asinine joke started behind the cashier's glasses, and changed to puzzlement when he looked at his assistant. The boy was rouge-red and the grin he was forcing his mouth to wear was a terrible thing.

Dritton cleared his throat and said heartily:

'It's a splendid morning. We've been having splendid weather.'

'But isn't there a private room where we can talk?' I insisted.

Dritton jumped nervously and questioned the boy:

'What – what is this?'

Young Albury said something nobody could have understood.

I said: 'If there isn't I'll have to take him down to the City Hall.'

Dritton caught his glasses as they slid down his nose, jammed them back in place and said:

'Come back here.'

We followed him down the length of the lobby, through a gate, and into an office whose door was labelled *President* – old Elihu's office. Nobody was in it.

I motioned Albury into one chair and picked another for myself. The cashier fidgeted with his back against the desk, facing both of us.

'Now, sir, will you explain this,' he said.

'We'll get around to that,' I told him and turned to the boy. 'You're an ex-boy-friend of Dinah's who was given the air. You're the only one who knew her intimately who could have known about the certified check in time to phone Mrs Willsson and Thaler. Willsson was shot with a .32. Banks like that caliber. Maybe the gun you used wasn't a bank gun, but I think it was. Maybe you didn't put it back. Then there'll be one missing. Anyway, I'm going to have a gun expert put his microscopes and micrometers on the bullets that killed Willsson and bullets fired from all the bank guns.'

The boy looked calmly at me and said nothing. He had himself under control again. That wouldn't do. I had to be nasty. I said:

'You were cuckoo over the girl. You confessed to me that it was only because she wouldn't stand for it that you didn't—'

'Don't – please don't,' he gasped. His face was red again.

I made myself sneer at him until his eyes went down. Then I said:

'You talked too much, son. You were too damned anxious to make your life an open book for me. That's a way you amateur criminals have. You've always got to overdo the frank and open business.'

He was watching his hands. I let him have the other barrel:

'You know you killed him. You know if you used a bank gun, and if you put it back. If you did you're nailed now, without an out. The gun-sharks will take care of that. If you didn't, I'm going to nail you anyhow. All right. I don't have to tell you whether you've got a chance or not. You know.

'Noonan is framing Whisper Thaler for the job. He can't convict him, but the frame-up is tight enough that if Thaler's killed resisting arrest, the chief will be in the clear. That's what he means to do – kill Thaler. Thaler stood off the police all night in his King Street joint. He's still standing them off – unless they've got to him. The first copper that gets to him – exit Thaler.

'If you figure you've got a chance to beat your rap, and you want to let another man be killed on your account, that's your business. But if you know you haven't got a chance – and you haven't if the gun can be found – for God's sake give Thaler one by clearing him.'

'I'd like,' Albury's voice was an old man's. He looked up from his hands, saw Dritton, said, 'I'd like,' again and stopped.

'Where is the gun?' I asked.

'In Harper's cage,' the boy said.

I scowled at the cashier and asked him:

'Will you get it?'

He went out as if he were glad to go.

'I didn't mean to kill him,' the youngster said. 'I don't think I meant to.'

I nodded encouragingly, trying to look solemnly sympathetic.

'I don't think I meant to kill him,' he repeated, 'though I took the gun with me. You were right about my being cuckoo over Dinah – then. It was worse some days than others. The day Willsson brought the check in was one of the bad ones. All I could think about was that I had lost her because I had no more money, and he was taking five thousand dollars to her. It was the check. Can you understand that? I had known that she and Thaler were – you know. If I had learned that Willsson and she were too, without seeing the check, I wouldn't have done anything. I'm sure of it. It was seeing the check – and knowing I'd lost her because my money was gone.

'I watched her house that night and saw him go in. I was afraid of what I might do, because it was one of the bad days, and I had the gun in my pocket. Honestly I didn't want to do anything. I was afraid. I couldn't think of anything but the check, and why I had lost her. I knew Willsson's wife was jealous. Everybody knew that. I thought if I called her up and told her – I don't know exactly what I thought, but I went to a store around the corner and phoned her. Then I phoned Thaler. I wanted them there. If I could have thought of anyone else who had anything to do with either Dinah or Willsson I'd have called them too.

'Then I went back and watched Dinah's house again. Mrs Willsson came, and then Thaler, and both of them stayed there, watching the house. I was glad of that. With them there I wasn't so afraid of what I might do. After a while Willsson came out and walked down the street. I looked up at Mrs Willsson's car and at the doorway where I knew Thaler was. Neither of them did anything, and Willsson was walking away. I knew then why I had wanted them there. I had hoped they would do something – and I wouldn't have to. But they didn't, and he was walking away. If one of them had gone over and said something to him, or even followed him, I wouldn't have done anything.

'But they didn't. I remember taking the gun out of my pocket. Everything was blurred in front of my eyes, like I was crying. Maybe I was. I don't remember shooting – I mean I don't remember deliberately aiming and pulling the trigger – but I can remember the sound the shots made, and that I knew the noise was coming from the gun in my hand. I don't remember how Willsson looked, if he fell before I turned and ran up the alley, or not. When I got home I cleaned and reloaded the pistol, and put it back in the paying teller's cage the next morning.'

*

On the way down to the City Hall with the boy and the gun I apologized for the village cut-up stuff I had put in the early part of the shake-down, explaining:

'I had to get under your skin, and that was the best way I knew. The way you'd talked about the girl showed me you were too good an actor to be broken down by straight hammering.'

He winced, and said slowly:

'That wasn't acting, altogether. When I was in danger, facing the gallows, she didn't – didn't seem so important to me. I couldn't – I can't now – quite understand – fully – why I did what I did. Do you know what I mean? That somehow makes the whole thing – and me – cheap. I mean, the whole thing from the beginning.'

I couldn't find anything to say except something meaningless, like:

'Things happen that way.'

In the chief's office we found one of the men who had been on the storming party the night before – a red-faced official named Biddle. He goggled at me with curious gray eyes, but asked no questions about the King Street doings.

Biddle called in a young lawyer named Dart from the prosecuting attorney's office. Albury was repeating his story to Biddle, Dart and a stenographer, when the chief of police, looking as if he had just crawled out of bed, arrived.

'Well, it certainly is fine to see you,' Noonan said, pumping my hand up and down while patting my back. 'By God! You had a narrow one last night – the rats! I was dead sure they'd got you till we kicked in the doors and found the joint empty. Tell me how those son-of-a-guns got out of there.'

'A couple of your men let them out the back door, took them through the house in back, and sent them away in a department car. They took me along so I couldn't tip you off.'

'A couple of my men did that?' he asked, with no appearance of surprise. 'Well, well! What kind of looking men were they?'

I described them.

'Shore and Riordan,' he said. 'I might of known it. Now what's all this?' nodding his fat face at Albury.

I told him briefly while the boy went on dictating his statement.

The chief chuckled and said:

'Well, well, I did Whisper an injustice. I'll have to hunt him up and square myself. So you landed the boy? That certainly is fine. Congratulations and thanks.' He shook my hand again. 'You'll not be leaving our city now, will you?'

'Not just yet.'

'That's fine,' he assured me.

I went out for breakfast-and-lunch. Then I treated myself to a shave and hair-cut, sent a telegram to the Agency asking to have Dick Foley and Mickey Linehan shipped to Personville, stopped in my room for a change of clothes, and set out for my client's house.

Old Elihu was wrapped in blankets in an armchair at a sunny window. He gave me a stubby hand and thanked me for catching his son's murderer.

I made some more or less appropriate reply. I didn't ask him how he had got the news.

'The check I gave you last night,' he said, 'is only fair pay for the work you have done.'

'Your son's check more than covered that.'

'Then call mine a bonus.'

'The Continental's got rules against taking bonuses or rewards,' I said.

His face began to redden.

'Well, damn it—'

'You haven't forgotten that your check was to cover the cost of investigating crime and corruption in Personville, have you?' I asked.

'That was nonsense,' he snorted. 'We were excited last night. That's called off.'

'Not with me.'

He threw a lot of profanity around. Then:

'It's my money and I won't have it wasted on a lot of damn-foolery. If you won't take it for what you've done, give it back to me.'

'Stop yelling at me,' I said. 'I'll give you nothing except a good job of city-cleaning. That's what you bargained for, and that's what you're going to get. You know now that your son was killed by young Albury, and not by your playmates. They know now that Thaler wasn't helping you double-cross them. With your son dead, you've been able to promise them that the newspapers won't dig up any more dirt. All's lovely and peaceful again.

'I told you I expected something like that. That's why I sewed you up. And you are sewed up. The check has been certified, so you can't stop payment. The letter of authority may not be as good as a contract, but you'll have to go into court to prove that it isn't. If you want that much of that kind of publicity, go ahead. I'll see that you get plenty.

'Your fat chief of police tried to assassinate me last night. I don't like that. I'm just mean enough to want to ruin him for it. Now I'm going to have my fun. I've got ten thousand dollars of your money to play with. I'm going to use it opening Poison-ville up from Adam's apple to ankles. I'll see that you get my reports as regularly as possible. I hope you enjoy them.'

And I went out of the house with his curses sizzling around my head.

# 8
# A Tip on Kid Cooper

I spent most of the afternoon writing my three days' reports on the Donald Willsson operation. Then I sat around, burned Fatimas, and thought about the Elihu Willsson operation until dinner time.

I went down to the hotel dining room and had just decided in favor of pounded rump steak with mushrooms when I heard myself being paged.

The boy took me to one of the lobby booths. Dinah Brand's lazy voice came out of the receiver:

'Max wants to see you. Can you drop in tonight?'

'Your place?'

'Yes.'

I promised to drop in and returned to the dining room and my meal. When I had finished eating I went up to my room, fifth floor front. I unlocked the door and went in, snapping on the light.

A bullet kissed a hole in the door-frame close to my noodle.

More bullets made more holes in door, door-frame and wall, but by that time I had carried my noodle into a safe corner, one out of line with the window.

Across the street, I knew, was a four-story office building with a roof a little above the level of my window. The roof would be dark. My light was on. There was no percentage in trying to peep out under those conditions.

I looked around for something to chuck at the light globe, found a Gideon Bible, and chucked it. The bulb popped apart, giving me darkness.

The shooting had stopped.

I crept to the window, kneeling with an eye to one of its lower corners. The roof across the street was dark and too high for me to see beyond its rim. Ten minutes of this one-eyed spying got me nothing except a kink in my neck.

I went to the phone and asked the girl to send the house copper up.

He was a portly, white-mustached man with the round undeveloped forehead of a child. He wore a too-small hat on the back of his head to show the forehead. His name was Keever. He got too excited over the shooting.

The hotel manager came in, a plump man with carefully controlled face, voice and manner. He didn't get excited at all. He took the this-is-unheard-of-but-not-really-serious-of-course attitude of a street fakir whose mechanical dingus flops during a demonstration.

We risked light, getting a new globe, and added up the bullet-holes. There were ten of them.

Policemen came, went, and returned to report no luck in picking up whatever trail there might have been. Noonan called up. He talked to the sergeant in charge of the police detail, and then to me.

'I just this minute heard about the shooting,' he said. 'Now who do you reckon would be after you like that?'

'I couldn't guess,' I lied.

'None of them touched you?'

'No.'

'Well, that certainly is fine,' he said heartily. 'And we'll nail that baby, whoever he was, you can bet your life on that. Would you like me to leave a couple of the boys with you, just to see nothing else happens?'

'No, thanks.'

'You can have them if you want them,' he insisted.

'No, thanks.'

He made me promise to call on him the first chance I got, told me the Personville police department was at my disposal, gave me to understand that if anything happened to me his whole life would be ruined, and I finally got rid of him.

The police went away. I had my stuff moved into another room, one into which bullets couldn't be so easily funneled. Then I changed my clothes and set out for Hurricane Street, to keep my date with the whispering gambler.

Dinah Brand opened the door for me. Her big ripe mouth was rouged evenly this evening, but her brown hair still needed trimming, was parted haphazardly, and there were spots down the front of her orange silk dress.

'So you're still alive,' she said. 'I suppose nothing can be done about it. Come on in.'

We went into her cluttered-up living room. Dan Rolff and Max Thaler were playing pinochle there. Rolff nodded to me. Thaler got up to shake hands.

His hoarse whispering voice said:

'I hear you've declared war on Poisonville.'

'Don't blame me. I've got a client who wants the place ventilated.'

'Wanted, not wants,' he corrected me as we sat down. 'Why don't you chuck it?'

I made a speech:

'No. I don't like the way Poisonville has treated me. I've got my chance now, and I'm going to even up. I take it you're back in the club again, all brothers together, let bygones be bygones. You want to be let alone. There was a time when I wanted to be let alone. If I had been, maybe now I'd be riding back to San

Francisco. But I wasn't. Especially I wasn't let alone by that fat Noonan. He's had two tries at my scalp in two days. That's plenty. Now it's my turn to run him ragged, and that's exactly what I'm going to do. Poisonville is ripe for the harvest. It's a job I like, and I'm going to do it.'

'While you last,' the gambler said.

'Yeah,' I agreed. 'I was reading in the paper this morning about a fellow choking to death eating a chocolate eclair in bed.'

'That may be good,' said Dinah Brand, her big body sprawled in an arm-chair, 'but it wasn't in this morning's paper.'

She lit a cigarette and threw the match out of sight under the chesterfield. The lunger had gathered up the cards and was shuffling them over and over, purposelessly.

Thaler frowned at me and said:

'Willsson's willing for you to keep the ten grand. Let it go at that.'

'I've got a mean disposition. Attempted assassinations make me mad.'

'That won't get you anything but a box. I'm for you. You kept Noonan from framing me. That's why I'm telling you, forget it and go back to Frisco.'

'I'm for you,' I said. 'That's why I'm telling you, split with them. They crossed you up once. It'll happen again. Anyway, they're slated for the chutes. Get out while the getting's good.'

'I'm sitting too pretty,' he said. 'And I'm able to take care of myself.'

'Maybe. But you know the racket's too good to last. You've had the cream of the pickings. Now it's get-away day.'

He shook his little dark head and told me:

'I think you're pretty good, but I'm damned if I think you're good enough to crack this camp. It's too tight. If I thought you could swing it, I'd be with you. You know how I stand with Noonan. But you'll never make it. Chuck it.'

'No. I'm in it to the last nickel of Elihu's ten thousand.'

'I told you he was too damned pig-headed to listen to reason,' Dinah Brand said, yawning. 'Isn't there anything to drink in the dump, Dan?'

The lunger got up from the table and went out of the room.

Thaler shrugged, said:

'Have it your way. You're supposed to know what you're doing. Going to the fights tomorrow night?'

I said I thought I would. Dan Rolff came in with gin and trimmings. We had a couple of drinks apiece. We talked about the fights. Nothing more was said about me versus Poisonville. The gambler apparently had washed his hands of me, but he didn't seem to hold my stubbornness against me. He even gave me what seemed to be a straight tip on the fights – telling me any bet on the main event would be good if its maker remembered that Kid Cooper would probably knock Ike Bush out in the sixth round. He seemed to know what he was talking about, and it didn't seem to be news to the others.

I left a little after eleven, returning to the hotel without anything happening.

# 9
# A Black Knife

I woke next morning with an idea in my skull. Personville had only some forty thousand inhabitants. It shouldn't be hard to spread news. Ten o'clock found me out spreading it.

I did my spreading in pool rooms, cigar stores, speakeasies, soft drink joints, and on street corners – wherever I found a man or two loafing. My spreading technique was something like this:

'Got a match? . . . Thanks . . . Going to the fights to-night? . . . I hear Ike Bush takes a dive in the sixth . . . It ought to be straight: I got it from Whisper . . . Yeah, they all are.'

People like inside stuff, and anything that had Thaler's name to it was very inside in Personville. The news spread nicely. Half the men I gave it to worked almost as hard as I did spreading it, just to show they knew what was what.

When I started out, seven to four was being offered that Ike Bush would win, and two to three that he would win by a knock-out. By two o'clock none of the joints taking bets were offering anything better than even money, and by half-past three Kid Cooper was a two-to-one favorite.

I made my last stop a lunch counter, where I tossed the news out to a waiter and a couple of customers while eating a hot beef sandwich.

When I went out I found a man waiting by the door for me. He had bowed legs and a long sharp jaw, like a hog's. He nodded and walked down the street beside me, chewing a toothpick and squinting sidewise into my face. At the corner he said:

'I know for a fact that ain't so.'

'What?' I asked.

'About Ike Bush flopping. I know for a fact that ain't so.'

'Then it oughtn't bother you any. But the wise money's going two to one on Cooper, and he's not that good unless Bush lets him be.'

The hog jaw spit out the mangled toothpick and snapped yellow teeth at me.

'He told me his own self that Cooper was a set-up for him, last night, and he wouldn't do nothing like that – not to me.'

'Friend of yours?'

'Not exactly, but he knows I— Hey, listen! Did Whisper give you that, on the level?'

'On the level.'

He cursed bitterly. 'And I put my last thirty-five bucks in the world on that rat on his say-so. Me, that could send him over for—' He broke off and looked down the street.

'Could send him over for what?' I asked.

'Plenty,' he said. 'Nothing.'

I had a suggestion:

'If you've got something on him, maybe we ought to talk it over. I wouldn't mind seeing Bush win, myself. If what you've got is any good, what's the matter with putting it up to him?'

He looked at me, at the sidewalk, fumbled in his vest pocket for another toothpick, put it in his mouth, and mumbled:

'Who are you?'

I gave him a name, something like Hunter or Hunt or Huntington, and asked him his. He said his name was Mac-

Swain, Bob MacSwain, and I could ask anybody in town if it wasn't right.

I said I believed him and asked:

'What do you say? Will we put the squeeze to Bush?'

Little hard lights came into his eyes and died.

'No,' he gulped. 'I ain't that kind of fellow. I never—'

'You never did anything but let people gyp you. You don't have to go up against him, MacSwain. Give me the dope, and I'll make the play – if it's any good.'

He thought that over, licking his lips, letting the toothpick fall down to stick on his coat front.

'You wouldn't let on about me having any part in it?' he asked. 'I belong here, and I wouldn't stand a chance if it got out. And you won't turn him up? You'll just use it to make him fight?'

'Right.'

He took my hand excitedly and demanded:

'Honest to God?'

'Honest to God.'

'His real moniker is Al Kennedy. He was in on the Keystone Trust knock-over in Philly two years ago, when Scissors Haggerty's mob croaked two messengers. Al didn't do the killing, but he was in on the caper. He used to scrap around Philly. The rest of them got copped, but he made the sneak. That's why he's sticking out here in the bushes. That's why he won't never let them put his mug in the papers or on any cards. That's why he's a pork-and-beaner when he's as good as the best. See? This Ike Bush is Al Kennedy that the Philly bulls want for the Keystone trick. See? He was in on the—'

'I see. I see,' I stopped the merry-go-round. 'The next thing is to go to see him. How do we do that?'

'He flops at the Maxwell, on Union Street. I guess maybe he'd be there now, resting up for the mill.'

'Resting for what? He doesn't know he's going to fight. We'll give it a try, though.'

'We! We! Where do you get that *we* at? You said – you swore you'd keep me covered.'

'Yeah,' I said, 'I remember that now. What does he look like?'

'A black-haired kid, kind of slim, with one tin ear and eyebrows that run straight across. I don't know if you can make him like it.'

'Leave that to me. Where'll I find you afterwards?'

'I'll be hanging around Murry's. Mind you don't tip my mitt. You promised.'

The Maxwell was one of a dozen hotels along Union Street with narrow front doors between stores, and shabby stairs leading up to second-story offices. The Maxwell's office was simply a wide place in the hall, with a key- and mail-rack behind a wooden counter that needed paint just as badly. A brass bell and a dirty day-book register were on the counter. Nobody was there.

I had to run back eight pages before I found *Ike Bush, Salt Lake City, 214*, written in the book. The pigeon-hole that had that number was empty. I climbed more steps and knocked on a door that had it. Nothing came of that. I tried it two or three times more and then turned back to the stairs.

Somebody was coming up. I stood at the top, waiting for a look at him. There was just light enough to see by.

He was a slim muscular lad in army shirt, blue suit, gray cap. Black eyebrows made a straight line above his eyes.

I said: 'Hello.'

He nodded without stopping or saying anything.

'Win tonight?' I asked.

'Hope so,' he said shortly, passing me.

I let him take four steps toward his room before I told him:

'So do I. I'd hate to have to ship you back to Philly, Al.'

He took another step, turned around very slowly, rested a shoulder against the wall, let his eyes get sleepy, and grunted:

'Huh?'

'If you were smacked down in the sixth or any other round by a palooka like Kid Cooper, it'd make me peevish,' I said. 'Don't do it, Al. You don't want to go back to Philly.'

The youngster put his chin down in his neck and came back to me. When he was within arm's reach, he stopped, letting his left side turn a bit to the front. His hands were hanging loose. Mine were in my overcoat pockets.

He said, 'Huh?' again.

I said:

'Try to remember that – if Ike Bush doesn't turn in a win tonight, Al Kennedy will be riding east in the morning.'

He lifted his left shoulder an inch. I moved the gun around in my pocket, enough. He grumbled:

'Where do you get that stuff about me not winning?'

'Just something I heard. I didn't think there was anything in it, except maybe a ducat back to Philly.'

'I oughta bust your jaw, you fat crook.'

'Now's the time to do it,' I advised him. 'If you win tonight you're not likely to see me again. If you lose, you'll see me, but your hands won't be loose.'

I found MacSwain in Murry's, a Broadway pool room.

'Did you get to him?' he asked.

'Yeah. It's all fixed – if he doesn't blow town, or say something to his backers, or just pay no attention to me, or—'

MacSwain developed a lot of nervousness.

'You better damn sight be careful,' he warned me. 'They might try to put you out of the way. He— I got to see a fellow down the street,' and he deserted me.

Poisonville's prize fighting was done in a big wooden ex-casino in what had once been an amusement park on the edge of town. When I got there at eight-thirty, most of the population seemed to be on hand, packed tight in close rows of folding chairs on the main floor, packed tighter on benches in two dinky balconies.

Smoke. Stink. Heat. Noise.

My seat was in the third row, ringside. Moving down to it, I discovered Dan Rolff in an aisle seat not far away, with Dinah Brand beside him. She had her hair trimmed at last, and marcelled, and looked like a lot of money in a big gray fur coat.

'Get down on Cooper?' she asked after we had swapped hellos.

'No. You playing him heavy?'

'Not as heavy as I'd like. We held off, thinking the odds would get better, but they went to hell.'

'Everybody in town seems to know Bush is going to dive,' I said. 'I saw a hundred put on Cooper at four to one a few minutes ago.' I leaned past Rolff and put my mouth close to where the gray fur collar hid the girl's ear, whispering: 'The dive is off. Better copper your bets while there's time.'

Her big bloodshot eyes went wide and dark with anxiety, greed, curiosity, suspicion.

'You mean it?' she asked huskily.

'Yeah.'

She chewed her reddened lips, frowned, asked:

'Where'd you get it?'

I wouldn't say. She chewed her mouth some more and asked:

'Is Max on?'

'I haven't seen him. Is he here?'

'I suppose so,' she said absent-mindedly, a distant look in her eyes. Her lips moved as if she were counting to herself.

I said: 'Take it or leave it, but it's a gut.'

She leaned forward to look sharply into my eyes, clicked her teeth together, opened her bag, and dragged out a roll of bills the size of a coffee can. Part of the roll she pushed at Rolff.

'Here, Dan, get it down on Bush. You've got an hour anyway to look over the odds.'

Rolff took the money and went off on his errand. I took his seat. She put a hand on my forearm and said:

'Christ help you if you've made me drop that dough.'

I pretended the idea was ridiculous.

The preliminary bouts got going, four-round affairs between assorted hams. I kept looking for Thaler, but couldn't see him. The girl squirmed beside me, paying little attention to the fighting, dividing her time between asking me where I had got my information and threatening me with hell-fire and damnation if it turned out to be a bust.

The semi-final was on when Rolff came back and gave the girl a handful of tickets. She was straining her eyes over them when I left for my own seat. Without looking up she called to me:

'Wait outside for us when it's over.'

Kid Cooper climbed into the ring while I was squeezing through to my seat. He was a ruddy straw-haired solid-built boy with a dented face and too much meat around the top of his lavender trunks. Ike Bush, alias Al Kennedy, came through the ropes in the opposite corner. His body looked better – slim, nicely ridged, snaky – but his face was pale, worried.

They were introduced, went to the center of the ring for the usual instructions, returned to their corners, shed bathrobes, stretched on the ropes, the gong rang, and the scrap was on.

Cooper was a clumsy bum. He had a pair of wide swings that might have hurt when they landed, but anybody with two feet could have kept away from them. Bush had class – nimble legs, a smooth fast left hand, and a right that got away quick. It would have been murder to put Cooper in the ring with the slim boy if he had been trying. But he wasn't. That is, he wasn't trying to win. He was trying not to, and had his hands full doing it.

Cooper waddled flat-footed around the ring, throwing his wide swings at everything from the lights to the corner posts. His system was simply to turn them loose and let them take their chances. Bush moved in and out, putting a glove on the ruddy boy whenever he wanted to, but not putting anything in the glove.

The customers were booing before the first round was over.

The second round was just as sour. I didn't feel so good. Bush didn't seem to have been much influenced by our little conversation. Out of the corner of my eye I could see Dinah Brand trying to catch my attention. She looked hot. I took care not to have my attention caught.

The room-mate act in the ring was continued in the third round to the tune of yelled Throw-em-outs, Why-don't-you-kiss-hims and Make-em-fights from the seats. The pugs' waltz brought them around to the corner nearest me just as the booing broke off for a moment.

I made a megaphone of my hands and bawled:

'Back to Philly, Al.'

Bush's back was to me. He wrestled Cooper around, shoving him into the ropes, so he – Bush – faced my way.

From somewhere far back in another part of the house another yelling voice came:

'Back to Philly, Al.'

MacSwain, I supposed.

A drunk off to one side lifted his puffy face and bawled the same thing, laughing as if it were a swell joke. Others took up the cry for no reason at all except that it seemed to disturb Bush.

His eyes jerked from side to side under the black bar of his eyebrows.

One of Cooper's wild mitts clouted the slim boy on the side of the jaw.

Ike Bush piled down at the referee's feet.

The referee counted five in two seconds, but the gong cut him off.

I looked over at Dinah Brand and laughed. There wasn't anything else to do. She looked at me and didn't laugh. Her face was sick as Dan Rolff's, but angrier.

Bush's handlers dragged him into his corner and rubbed him up, not working very hard at it. He opened his eyes and watched his feet. The gong was tapped.

Kid Cooper paddled out hitching up his trunks. Bush waited

until the bum was in the center of the ring, and then came to him, fast.

Bush's left glove went down, out – practically out of sight in Cooper's belly. Cooper said, 'Ugh,' and backed away, folding up.

Bush straightened him with a right-hand poke in the mouth, and sank the left again. Cooper said, 'Ugh,' again and had trouble with his knees.

Bush cuffed him once on each side of the head, cocked his right, carefully pushed Cooper's face into position with a long left, and threw his right hand straight from under his jaw to Cooper's.

Everybody in the house felt the punch.

Cooper hit the floor, bounced, and settled there. It took the referee half a minute to count ten seconds. It would have been just the same if he had taken half an hour. Kid Cooper was out.

When the referee had finally stalled through the count, he raised Bush's hand. Neither of them looked happy.

A high twinkle of light caught my eye. A short silvery streak slanted down from one of the small balconies.

A woman screamed.

The silvery streak ended its flashing slant in the ring, with a sound that was partly a thud, partly a snap.

Ike Bush took his arm out of the referee's hand and pitched down on top of Kid Cooper. A black knife-handle stuck out of the nape of Bush's neck.

# 10
# Crime Wanted – Male or Female

Half an hour later, when I left the building, Dinah Brand was sitting at the wheel of a pale blue little Marmon, talking to Max Thaler, who stood in the road.

The girl's square chin was tilted up. Her big red mouth was brutal around the words it shaped, and the lines crossing its ends were deep, hard.

The gambler looked as unpleasant as she. His pretty face was yellow and tough as oak. When he talked his lips were paper-thin.

It seemed to be a nice family party. I wouldn't have joined it if the girl hadn't seen me and called:

'My God, I thought you were never coming.'

I went over to the car. Thaler looked across the hood at me with no friendliness at all.

'Last night I advised you to go back to Frisco.' His whisper was harsher than anybody's shout could have been. 'Now I'm telling you.'

'Thanks just the same,' I said as I got in beside the girl.

While she was stirring the engine up he said to her:

'This isn't the first time you've sold me out. It's the last.'

She put the car in motion, turned her head back over her shoulder, and sang to him:

'To hell, my love, with you!'

We rode into town rapidly.

'Is Bush dead?' she asked as she twisted the car into Broadway.

'Decidedly. When they turned him over the point of the knife was sticking out in front.'

'He ought to have known better than to double-cross them. Let's get something to eat. I'm almost eleven hundred ahead on the night's doings, so if the boy friend doesn't like it, it's just too bad. How'd you come out?'

'Didn't bet. So your Max doesn't like it?'

'Didn't bet?' she cried. 'What kind of an ass are you? Whoever heard of anybody not betting when they had a thing like that sewed up?'

'I wasn't sure it was sewed up. So Max didn't like the way things turned out?'

'You guessed it. He dropped plenty. And then he gets sore with me because I had sense enough to switch over and get in on the win.' She stopped the car violently in front of a Chinese restaurant. 'The hell with him, the little tin-horn runt!'

Her eyes were shiny because they were wet. She jabbed a handkerchief into them as we got out of the car.

'My God, I'm hungry,' she said, dragging me across the sidewalk. 'Will you buy me a ton of *chow mein?*'

She didn't eat a ton of it, but she did pretty well, putting away a piled-up dish of her own and half of mine. Then we got back into the Marmon and rode out to her house.

Dan Rolff was in the dining room. A water glass and a brown bottle with no label stood on the table in front of him. He sat straight up in his chair, staring at the bottle. The room smelled of laudanum.

Dinah Brand slid her fur coat off, letting it fall half on a chair and half on the floor, and snapped her fingers at the lunger, saying impatiently:

'Did you collect?'

Without looking up from the bottle, he took a pad of paper money out of his inside pocket and dropped it on the table. The girl grabbed it, counted the bills twice, smacked her lips, and stuffed the money in her bag.

She went out to the kitchen and began chopping ice. I sat down and lit a cigarette. Rolff stared at his bottle. He and I never seemed to have much to say to one another. Presently the girl brought in some gin, lemon juice, seltzer and ice.

We drank and she told Rolff:

'Max is sore as hell. He heard you'd been running around putting last-minute money on Bush, and the little monkey thinks I double-crossed him. What did I have to do with it? All I did was what any sensible person would have done – get it on the win. I didn't have any more to do with it than a baby, did I?' she asked me.

'No.'

'Of course not. What's the matter with Max is he's afraid the others will think he was in on it too, that Dan was putting his dough down as well as mine. Well, that's his hard luck. He can go climb trees for all I care, the lousy little runt. Another drink would go good.'

She poured another for herself and for me. Rolff hadn't touched his first one. He said, still staring at the brown bottle:

'You can hardly expect him to be hilarious about it.'

The girl scowled and said disagreeably:

'I can expect anything I want. And he's got no right to talk to me that way. He doesn't own me. Maybe he thinks he does, but I'll show him different.' She emptied her glass, banged it on the table, and twisted around in her chair to face me. 'Is that on the level about your having ten thousand dollars of Elihu Willsson's money to use cleaning up the city?'

'Yeah.'

Her bloodshot eyes glistened hungrily.

'And if I help you will I get some of the ten—?'

'You can't do that, Dinah.' Rolff's voice was thick, but gently firm, as if he were talking to a child. 'That would be utterly filthy.'

The girl turned her face slowly toward him. Her mouth took on the look it had worn while talking to Thaler.

'I am going to do it,' she said. 'That makes me utterly filthy, does it?'

He didn't say anything, didn't look up from the bottle. Her face got red, hard, cruel. Her voice was soft, cooing:

'It's just too bad that a gentleman of your purity, even if he is a bit consumptive, has to associate with a filthy bum like me.'

'That can be remedied,' he said slowly, getting up. He was laudanumed to the scalp.

Dinah Brand jumped out of her chair and ran around the table to him. He looked at her with blank dopey eyes. She put her face close to his and demanded:

'So I'm too utterly filthy for you now, am I?'

He said evenly:

'I said to betray your friends to this chap would be utterly filthy, and it would.'

She caught one of his thin wrists and twisted it until he was on his knees. Her other hand, open, beat his hollow-cheeked face, half a dozen times on each side, rocking his head from side to side. He could have put his free arm up to protect his face, but didn't.

She let go his wrist, turned her back to him, and reached for gin and seltzer. She was smiling. I didn't like the smile.

He got up, blinking. His wrist was red where she had held it, his face bruised. He steadied himself upright and looked at me with dull eyes.

With no change in the blankness of his face and eyes, he put a hand under his coat, brought out a black automatic pistol, and fired at me.

But he was too shaky for either speed or accuracy. I had time to toss a glass at him. The glass hit his shoulder. His bullet went somewhere overhead.

I jumped before he got the next one out – jumped at him – was close enough to knock the gun down. The second slug went into the floor.

I socked his jaw. He fell away from me and lay where he fell.

I turned around.

Dinah Brand was getting ready to bat me over the head with the seltzer bottle, a heavy glass siphon that would have made pulp of my skull.

'Don't,' I yelped.

'You didn't have to bust him like that,' she snarled.

'Well, it's done. You'd better get him straightened out.'

She put down the siphon and I helped her carry him up to his bedroom. When he began moving his eyes, I left her to finish the work and went down to the dining room again. She joined me there fifteen minutes later.

'He's all right,' she said. 'But you could have handled him without that.'

'Yeah, but I did that for him. Know why he took the shot at me?'

'So I'd have nobody to sell Max out to?'

'No. Because I'd seen you maul him around.'

'That doesn't make sense to me,' she said. 'I was the one who did it.'

'He's in love with you, and this isn't the first time you've done it. He acted like he had learned there was no use matching muscle with you. But you can't expect him to enjoy having another man see you slap his face.'

'I used to think I knew men,' she complained, 'but, by God! I don't. They're lunatics, all of them.'

'So I poked him to give him back some of his self-respect. You know, treated him as I would a man instead of a down-and-outer who could be slapped around by girls.'

'Anything you say,' she sighed. 'I give up. We ought to have a drink.'

We had the drink, and I said:

'You were saying you'd work with me if there was a cut of the Willsson money in it for you. There is.'

'How much?'

'Whatever you earn. Whatever what you do is worth.'

'That's uncertain.'

'So's your help, so far as I know.'

'Is it? I can give you the stuff, brother, loads of it, and don't think I can't. I'm a girl who knows her Poisonville.' She looked down at her gray-stockinged knees, waved one leg at me, and exclaimed indignantly: 'Look at that. Another run. Did you ever see anything to beat it? Honest to God! I'm going bare-foot.'

'Your legs are too big,' I told her. 'They put too much strain on the material.'

'That'll do out of you. What's your idea of how to go about purifying our village?'

'If I haven't been lied to, Thaler, Pete the Finn, Lew Yard and Noonan are the men who've made Poisonville the sweet-smelling mess it is. Old Elihu comes in for his share of the blame, too, but it's not all his fault, maybe. Besides, he's my client, even if he doesn't want to be, so I'd like to go easy on him.

'The closest I've got to an idea is to dig up any and all the dirty work I can that might implicate the others, and run it out. Maybe I'll advertise – *Crime Wanted – Male or Female*. If they're as crooked as I think they are I shouldn't have a lot of trouble finding a job or two that I can hang on them.'

'Is that what you were up to when you uncooked the fight?'

'That was only an experiment – just to see what would happen.'

'So that's the way you scientific detectives work. My God! for a fat, middle-aged, hard-boiled, pig-headed guy, you've got the vaguest way of doing things I ever heard of.'

'Plans are all right sometimes,' I said. 'And sometimes just stirring things up is all right – if you're tough enough to survive, and keep your eyes open so you'll see what you want when it comes to the top.'

'That ought to be good for another drink,' she said.

# 11
# The Swell Spoon

We had another drink.

She put her glass down, licked her lips, and said:

'If stirring things up is your system, I've got a swell spoon for you. Did you ever hear of Noonan's brother Tim, the one who committed suicide out at Mock Lake a couple of years ago?'

'No.'

'You wouldn't have heard much good. Anyway, he didn't commit suicide. Max killed him.'

'Yeah?'

'For God's sake wake up. This I'm giving you is real. Noonan was like a father to Tim. Take the proof to him and he'll be after Max like nobody's business. That's what you want, isn't it?'

'We've got proof?'

'Two people got to Tim before he died, and he told them Max had done it. They're both still in town, though one won't live a lot longer. How's that?'

She looked as if she were telling the truth, though with women, especially blue-eyed women, that doesn't always mean anything.

'Let's listen to the rest of it,' I said. 'I like details and things.'

'You'll get them. You ever been out to Mock Lake? Well, it's our summer resort, thirty miles up the canyon road. It's a dump, but it's cool in summer, so it gets a good play. This was summer a year ago, the last week-end in August. I was out there with a fellow named Holly. He's back in England now, but you don't care anything about that, because he's got nothing to do with it. He was a funny sort of old woman – used to wear white silk socks turned inside out so the loose threads wouldn't hurt his feet. I got a letter from him last week. It's around here somewhere, but that doesn't make any difference.

'We were up there, and Max was up there with a girl he used to play around with – Myrtle Jennison. She's in the hospital now – City – dying of Bright's disease or something. She was a classy looking kid then, a slender blonde. I always liked her, except that a few drinks made her too noisy. Tim Noonan was crazy about her, but she couldn't see anybody but Max that summer.

'Tim wouldn't let her alone. He was a big good-looking Irishman, but a sap and a cheap crook who only got by because his brother was chief of police. Wherever Myrtle went, he'd pop up sooner or later. She didn't like to say anything to Max about it, not wanting Max to do anything to put him in wrong with Tim's brother, the chief.

'So of course Tim showed up at Mock Lake this Saturday. Myrtle and Max were just by themselves. Holly and I were with a bunch, but I saw Myrtle to talk to and she told me she had got a note from Tim, asking her to meet him for a few minutes that night, in one of the little arbor things on the hotel grounds. He said if she didn't he would kill himself. That was a laugh for us – the big false alarm. I tried to talk Myrtle out of going, but she had just enough booze in her to feel gay and she said she was going to give him an earful.

'We were all dancing in the hotel that night. Max was there for a while, and then I didn't see him any more. Myrtle was dancing with a fellow named Rutgers, a lawyer here in town. After a while she left him and went out one of the side doors. She winked at me when she passed, so I knew she was going down to see Tim. She had just got out when I heard the shot. Nobody else paid any attention to it. I suppose I wouldn't have noticed it either if I hadn't known about Myrtle and Tim.

'I told Holly I wanted to see Myrtle, and went out after her, by myself. I must have been about five minutes behind her in getting out. When I got outside I saw lights down by one of the summer houses, and people. I went down there, and— This talking is thirsty work.'

I poured out a couple of hookers of gin. She went into the kitchen for another siphon and more ice. We mixed them up, drank, and she settled down to her tale again:

'There was Tim Noonan, dead, with a hole in his temple and his gun lying beside him. Perhaps a dozen people were standing around, hotel people, visitors, one of Noonan's men, a dick named MacSwain. As soon as Myrtle saw me she took me away from the crowd, back in the shade of some trees.

' "Max killed him," she said. "What'll I do?"

'I asked her about it. She told me she had seen the flash of the gun and at first she thought Tim had killed himself after all. She was too far away and it was too dark for her to see anything else. When she ran down to him, he was rolling around, moaning, "He didn't have to kill me over her. I'd have—" She couldn't make out the rest of it. He was rolling around, bleeding from the hole in his temple.

'Myrtle was afraid Max had done it, but she had to be sure, so she knelt down and tried to pick up Tim's head, asking: "Who did it, Tim?"

'He was almost gone, but before he passed out he got enough strength to tell her, "Max!"

'She kept asking me, "What'll I do?" I asked her if anybody else had heard Tim, and she said the dick had. He came running up while she was trying to lift Tim's head. She didn't think anybody else had been near enough to hear, but the dick had.

'I didn't want Max to get in a jam over killing a mutt like Tim Noonan. Max didn't mean anything to me then, except that I liked him, and I didn't like any of the Noonans. I knew the dick – MacSwain. I used to know his wife. He had been a pretty good guy, straight as ace-deuce-trey-four-five, till he got on the force. Then he went the way of the rest of them. His wife stood as much of it as she could and then left him.

'Knowing this dick, I told Myrtle I thought we could fix things. A little jack would ruin MacSwain's memory, or, if he didn't like that, Max could have him knocked off. She had Tim's note threatening suicide. If the dick would play along, the hole in Tim's head from his own gun and the note would smooth everything over pretty.

'I left Myrtle under the trees and went out to hunt for Max. He wasn't around. There weren't many people there, and I could hear the hotel orchestra still playing dance music. I couldn't find Max, so I went back to Myrtle. She was all worked up over another idea. She didn't want Max to know that she had found out that he had killed Tim. She was afraid of him.

'See what I mean? She was afraid that if she and Max ever broke off he'd put her out of the way if he knew she had enough on him to swing him. I know how she felt. I got the same notion later, and kept just as quiet as she did. So we figured that if it could be fixed up without his knowing about it, so much the better. I didn't want to show in it either.

'Myrtle went back alone to the group around Tim and got hold of MacSwain. She took him off a little way and made the deal with him. She had some dough on her. She gave him two hundred and a diamond ring that had cost a fellow named Boyle a thousand. I thought he'd be back for more later, but he wasn't. He shot square with her. With the help of the letter he put over the suicide story.

'Noonan knew there was something fishy about the layout,

but he could never peg it. It think he suspected Max of having something to do with it. But Max had an air-tight alibi – trust him for that – and I think even Noonan finally counted him out. But Noonan never believed it happened the way it was made to look. He broke MacSwain – kicked him off the force.

'Max and Myrtle slid apart a little while after that. No row or anything – they just slid apart. I don't think she ever felt easy around him again, though so far as I know he never suspected her of knowing anything. She's sick now, as I told you, and hasn't got long to live. I think she'd not so much mind telling the truth if she were asked. MacSwain's still hanging around town. He'd talk if there was something in it for him. Those two have got the stuff on Max – and wouldn't Noonan eat it up! Is that good enough to give your stirring-up a start?'

'Couldn't it have been suicide?' I asked. 'With Tim Noonan getting a last-minute bright idea to stick it on Max?'

'That four-flusher shoot himself? Not a chance.'

'Could Myrtle have shot him?'

'Noonan didn't overlook that one. But she couldn't have been a third of the distance down the slope when the shot was fired. Tim had powder-marks on his head, and hadn't been shot and rolled down the slope. Myrtle's out.'

'But Max had an alibi?'

'Yes, indeed. He always has. He was in the hotel bar, on the other side of the building, all the time. Four men said so. As I remember it, they said it openly and often, long before anybody asked them. There were other men in the bar who didn't remember whether Max had been there or not, but those four remembered. They'd remember anything Max wanted remembered.'

Her eyes got large and then narrowed to black-fringed slits. She leaned toward me, upsetting her glass with an elbow.

'Peak Murry was one of the four. He and Max are on the outs now. Peak might tell it straight now. He's got a pool room on Broadway.'

'This MacSwain, does he happen to be named Bob?' I asked. 'A bow-legged man with a long jaw like a hog's?'

'Yes. You know him?'

'By sight. What does he do now?'

'A small-time grifter. What do you think of the stack-up?'

'Not bad. Maybe I can use it.'

'Then let's talk scratch.'

I grinned at the greed in her eyes and said:

'Not just yet, sister. We'll have to see how it works out before we start scattering pennies around.'

She called me a damned nickel-nurser and reached for the gin.

'No more for me, thanks,' I told her, looking at my watch. 'It's getting along toward five a.m. and I've got a busy day ahead.'

She decided she was hungry again. That reminded me that I was. It took a half an hour or more to get waffles, ham and coffee off the stove. It took some more time to get them into our stomachs and to smoke some cigarettes over extra cups of coffee. It was quite a bit after six when I got ready to leave.

I went back to my hotel and got into a tub of cold water. It braced me a lot, and I needed bracing. At forty I could get along on gin as a substitute for sleep, but not comfortably.

When I had dressed I sat down and composed a document:

Just before he died, Tim Noonan told me he had been shot by Max Thaler. Detective Bob MacSwain heard him tell me. I gave Detective MacSwain $200 and a diamond ring worth $1,000 to keep quiet and make it look like suicide.

With this document in my pocket I went downstairs, had another breakfast that was mostly coffee, and went up to the City Hospital.

Visiting hours were in the afternoon, but by flourishing my Continental Detective Agency credentials and giving everybody to understand that an hour's delay might cause thousands of deaths, or words to that effect, I got to see Myrtle Jennison.

She was in a ward on the third floor, alone. The other four beds were empty. She could have been a girl of twenty-five or a woman of fifty-five. Her face was a bloated spotty mask. Lifeless yellow hair in two stringy braids lay on the pillow beside her.

I waited until the nurse who had brought me up left. Then I held my document out to the invalid and said:

'Will you sign this, please, Miss Jennison?'

She looked at me with ugly eyes that were shaded into no particular dark color by the pads of flesh around them, then at the document, and finally brought a shapeless fat hand from under the covers to take it.

She pretended it took her nearly five minutes to read the forty-two words I had written. She let the document fall down on the covers and asked:

'Where'd you get that?' Her voice was tinny, irritable.

'Dinah Brand sent me to you.'

She asked eagerly:

'Has she broken off with Max?'

'Not that I know of,' I lied. 'I imagine she just wants to have this on hand in case it should come in handy.'

'And get her fool throat slit. Give me a pencil.'

I gave her my fountain pen and held my notebook under the document, to stiffen it while she scribbled her signature at the bottom, and to have it in my hands as soon as she had finished. While I fanned the paper dry she said:

'If that's what she wants it's all right with me. What do I care what anybody does now? I'm done. Hell with them all!' She sniggered and suddenly threw the bedclothes down to her knees, showing me a horrible swollen body in a coarse white nightgown. 'How do you like me? See, I'm done.'

I pulled the covers up over her again and said:

'Thanks for this, Miss Jennison.'

'That's all right. It's nothing to me any more. Only' – her puffy chin quivered – 'it's hell to die ugly as this.'

# 12

# A New Deal

I went out to hunt for MacSwain. Neither city directory nor telephone book told me anything. I did the pool rooms, cigar stores, speakeasies, looking around first, then asking cautious questions. That got me nothing. I walked the streets, looking for bowed legs. That got me nothing. I decided to go back to my hotel, grab a nap, and resume the hunting at night.

In a far corner of the lobby a man stopped hiding behind a newspaper and came out to meet me. He had bowed legs, a hog jaw, and was MacSwain.

I nodded carelessly at him and walked on toward the elevators. He followed me, mumbling:

'Hey, you got a minute?'

'Yeah, just about.' I stopped, pretending indifference.

'Let's get out of sight,' he said nervously.

I took him up to my room. He straddled a chair and put a match in his mouth. I sat on the side of the bed and waited for him to say something. He chewed his match a while and began:

'I'm going to come clean with you, brother. I'm—'

'You mean you're going to tell me you knew me when you braced me yesterday?' I asked. 'And you're going to tell me Bush hadn't told you to bet on him? And you didn't until afterwards?

And you knew about his record because you used to be a bull? And you thought if you could get me to put it to him you could clean up a little dough playing him?'

'I'll be damned if I was going to come through with that much,' he said, 'but since it's been said I'll put a yes to it.'

'Did you clean up?'

'I win myself six hundred iron men.' He pushed his hat back and scratched his forehead with the chewed end of his match. 'And then I lose myself that and my own two hundred and some in a crap game. What do you think of that? I pick up six hundred berries like shooting fish, and have to bum four bits for breakfast.'

I said it was a tough break but that was the kind of a world we lived in.

He said, 'Uh-huh,' put the match back in his mouth, ground it some more, and added: 'That's why I thought I'd come to see you. I used to be in the racket myself and—'

'What did Noonan put the skids under you for?'

'Skids? What skids? I quit. I come into a piece of change when the wife got killed in an automobile accident – insurance – and I quit.'

'I heard he kicked you out the time his brother shot himself.'

'Well, then you heard wrong. It was just after that, but you can ask him if I didn't quit.'

'It's not that much to me. Go on telling me why you came to see me.'

'I'm busted, flat. I know you're a Continental op, and I got a pretty good hunch what you're up to here. I'm close to a lot that's going on on both sides of things in this burg. There's things I could do for you, being an ex-dick, knowing the ropes both ways.'

'You want to stool-pigeon for me?'

He looked me straight in the eye and said evenly:

'There's no sense in a man picking out the worst name he can find for everything.'

'I'll give you something to do, MacSwain.' I took out Myrtle Jennison's document and passed it to him. 'Tell me about that.'

He read it through carefully, his lips framing the words, the match wavering up and down in his mouth. He got up, put the paper on the bed beside me, and scowled down at it.

'There's something I'll have to find out about first,' he said, very solemnly. 'I'll be back in a little while and give you the whole story.'

I laughed and told him:

'Don't be silly. You know I'm not going to let you walk out on me.'

'I don't know that.' He shook his head, still solemn: 'Neither do you. All you know is whether you're going to try to stop me.'

'The answer's yeah,' I said while I considered that he was fairly hard and strong, six or seven years younger than I, and twenty or thirty pounds lighter.

He stood at the foot of the bed and looked at me with solemn eyes. I sat on the side of the bed and looked at him with whatever kind of eyes I had at the time. We did this for nearly three minutes.

I used part of the time measuring the distance between us, figuring out how, by throwing my body back on the bed and turning on my hip, I could get my heels in his face if he jumped me. He was too close for me to pull the gun. I had just finished this mental map-making when he spoke:

'That lousy ring wasn't worth no grand. I did swell to get two centuries for it.'

He shook his head again and said:

'First I want to know what you're meaning to do about it.'

'Cop Whisper.'

'I don't mean that. I mean with me.'

'You'll have to go over to the Hall with me.'

'I won't.'

'Why not? You're only a witness.'

'I'm only a witness that Noonan can hang a bribe-taking, or

an accomplice after the act rap on, or both. And he'd be tickled simple to have the chance.'

This jaw-wagging didn't seem to be leading anywhere. I said:

'That's too bad. But you're going to see him.'

'Try and take me.'

I sat up straighter and slid my right hand back to my hip.

He grabbed for me. I threw my body back on the bed, did the hip-spin, swung my feet at him. It was a good trick, only it didn't work. In his hurry to get at me he bumped the bed aside just enough to spill me off on the floor.

I landed all sprawled out on my back. I kept dragging at my gun while I tried to roll under the bed.

Missing me, his lunge carried him over the low footboard, over the side of the bed. He came down beside me, on the back of his neck, his body somersaulting over.

I put the muzzle of my gun in his left eye and said:

'You're making a fine pair of clowns of us. Be still while I get up or I'll make an opening in your head for brains to leak in.'

I got up, found and pocketed my document, and let him get up.

'Knock the dents out of your hat and put your necktie in front, so you won't disgrace me going through the streets,' I ordered after I had run a hand over his clothes and found nothing that felt like a weapon. 'You can suit yourself about remembering that this gat is going to be in my overcoat pocket, with a hand on it.'

He straightened his hat and tie and said:

'Hey, listen: I'm in this, I guess, and cutting up won't get me nothing. Suppose I be good. Could you forget about the tussle? See – maybe it'd be smoother for me if they thought I come along without being dragged.'

'O.K.'

'Thanks, brother.'

Noonan was out eating. We had to wait half an hour in his

outer office. When he came in he greeted me with the usual *How are you? . . . That certainly is fine . . .* and the rest of it. He didn't say anything to MacSwain – simply eyed him sourly.

We went into the chief's private office. He pulled a chair over to his desk for me and then sat in his own, ignoring the ex-dick.

I gave Noonan the sick girl's document.

He gave it one glance, bounced out of his chair, and smashed a fist the size of a cantaloup into MacSwain's face.

The punch carried MacSwain across the room until a wall stopped him. The wall creaked under the strain, and a framed photograph of Noonan and other city dignitaries welcoming somebody in spats dropped down to the floor with the hit man.

The fat chief waddled over, picked up the picture and beat it to splinters on MacSwain's head and shoulders.

Noonan came back to his desk, puffing, smiling, saying cheerfully to me:

'That fellow's a rat if there ever was one.'

MacSwain sat up and looked around, bleeding from nose, mouth and head.

Noonan roared at him:

'Come here, you.'

MacSwain said, 'Yes, chief,' scrambled up and ran over to the desk.

Noonan said: 'Come through or I'll kill you.'

MacSwain said:

'Yes, chief. It was like she said, only that rock wasn't worth no grand. But she give me it and the two hundred to keep my mouth shut, because I got there just when she asks him, "Who did it, Tim?" and he says, "Max!" He says it kind of loud and sharp, like he wanted to get it out before he died, because he died right then, almost before he'd got it out. That's the way it was, chief, but the rock wasn't worth no—'

'Damn the rock,' Noonan barked. 'And stop bleeding on my rug.'

MacSwain hunted in his pocket for a dirty handkerchief, mopped his nose and mouth with it, and jabbered on:

'That's the way it was, chief. Everything else was like I said at the time, only I didn't say anything about hearing him say Max done it. I know I hadn't ought to—'

'Shut up,' Noonan said, and pressed one of the buttons on his desk.

A uniformed copper came in. The chief jerked a thumb at MacSwain and said:

'Take this baby down cellar and let the wrecking crew work on him before you lock him up.'

MacSwain started a desperate plea, 'Aw, chief!' but the copper took him away before he could get any farther.

Noonan stuck a cigar at me, tapped the document with another and asked:

'Where's this broad?'

'In the City Hospital, dying. You'll have the 'cuter get a stiff out of her? That one's not so good legally – I framed it for effect. Another thing – I hear that Peak Murry and Whisper aren't playmates any more. Wasn't Murry one of his alibis?'

The chief said, 'He was,' picked up one of his phones, said, 'McGraw,' and then: 'Get hold of Peak Murry and ask him to drop in. And have Tony Agosti picked up for that knife-throwing.'

He put the phone down, stood up, made a lot of cigar smoke, and said through it:

'I haven't always been on the up-and-up with you.'

I thought that was putting it mildly, but I didn't say anything while he went on:

'You know your way around. You know what these jobs are. There's this one and that one that's got to be listened to. Just because a man's chief of police doesn't mean he's chief. Maybe you're a lot of trouble to somebody that can be a lot of trouble to me. Don't make any difference if I think you're a right guy. I got to play with them that play with me. See what I mean?'

I wagged my head to show I did.

'That's the way it was,' he said. 'But no more. This is something else, a new deal. When the old woman kicked off Tim was just a lad. She said to me, "Take care of him, John,' and I promised I would. And then Whisper murders him on account of that tramp.' He reached down and took my hand. 'See what I'm getting at? That's a year and a half ago, and you give me my first chance to hang it on him. I'm telling you there's no man in Personville that's got a voice big enough to talk you down. Not after today.'

That pleased me and I said so. We purred at each other until a lanky man with an extremely up-turned nose in the middle of a round and freckled face was ushered in. It was Peak Murry.

'We were just wondering about the time when Tim died,' the chief said when Murry had been given a chair and a cigar, 'where Whisper was. You were out to the Lake that night, weren't you?'

'Yep,' Murry said and the end of his nose got sharper.

'With Whisper?'

'I wasn't with him all the time.'

'Were you with him at the time of the shooting?'

'Nope.'

The chief's greenish eyes got smaller and brighter. He asked softly:

'You know where he was?'

'Nope.'

The chief sighed in a thoroughly satisfied way and leaned back in his chair.

'Damn it, Peak,' he said, 'you told us before that you were with him at the bar.'

'Yep, I did,' the lanky man admitted. 'But that don't mean nothing except that he asked me to and I didn't mind helping out a friend.'

'Meaning you don't mind standing a perjury rap?'

'Don't kid me.' Murry spit vigorously at the cuspidor. 'I didn't say nothing in no court rooms.'

'How about Jerry and George Kelly and O'Brien?' the chief asked. 'Did they say they were with him just because he asked them to?'

'O'Brien did. I don't know nothing about the others. I was going out of the bar when I run into Whisper, Jerry and Kelly, and went back to have a shot with them. Kelly told me Tim had been knocked off. Then Whisper says, "It never hurts anybody to have an alibi. We were here all the time, weren't we?" and he looks at O'Brien, who's behind the bar. O'Brien says, "Sure you was," and when Whisper looks at me I say the same thing. But I don't know no reasons why I've got to cover him up nowadays.'

'And Kelly said Tim had been knocked off? Didn't say he had been found dead?'

' "Knocked off" was the words he used.'

The chief said:

'Thanks, Peak. You oughtn't to have done like you did, but what's done is done. How are the kids?'

Murry said they were doing fine, only the baby wasn't as fat as he'd like to have him. Noonan phoned the prosecuting attorney's office and had Dart and a stenographer take Peak's story before he left.

Noonan, Dart and the stenographer set out for the City Hospital to get a complete statement from Myrtle Jennison. I didn't go along. I decided I needed sleep, told the chief I would see him later, and returned to the hotel.

# 13
# – $200.10 –

had my vest unbuttoned when the telephone bell rang.

It was Dinah Brand, complaining that she had been trying to get me since ten o'clock.

'Have you done anything on what I told you?' she asked.

'I've been looking it over. It seems pretty good. I think maybe I'll crack it this afternoon.'

'Don't. Hold it till I see you. Can you come up now?'

I looked at the vacant white bed and said, 'Yes,' without much enthusiasm.

Another tub of cold water did me so little good that I almost fell asleep in it.

Dan Rolff let me in when I rang the girl's bell. He looked and acted as if nothing out of the ordinary had happened the night before. Dinah Brand came into the hall to help me off with my overcoat. She had on a tan woolen dress with a two-inch rip in one shoulder seam.

She took me into the living room. She sat on the chesterfield beside me and said:

'I'm going to ask you to do something for me. You like me enough, don't you?'

I admitted that. She counted the knuckles of my left hand with a warm forefinger and explained:

'I want you to not do anything more about what I told you last night. Now wait a minute. Wait till I get through. Dan was right. I oughtn't sell Max out like that. It would be utterly filthy. Besides, it's Noonan you chiefly want, isn't it? Well, if you'll be a nice darling and lay off Max this time, I'll give you enough on Noonan to nail him forever. You'd like that better, wouldn't you? And you like me too much to want to take advantage of me by using information I gave you when I was mad at what Max had said, don't you?'

'What is the dirt on Noonan?' I asked.

She kneaded my biceps and murmured: 'You promise?'

'Not yet.'

She pouted at me and said:

'I'm off Max for life, on the level. You've got no right to make me turn rat.'

'What about Noonan?'

'Promise first.'

'No.'

She dug fingers into my arm and asked sharply:

'You've already gone to Noonan?'

'Yeah.'

She let go my arm, frowned, shrugged, and said gloomily:

'Well, how can I help it?'

I stood up and a voice said:

'Sit down.'

It was a hoarse whispering voice – Thaler's.

I turned to see him standing in the dining room doorway, a big gun in one of his little hands. A red-faced man with a scarred cheek stood behind him.

The other doorway – opening to the hall – filled as I sat down. The loose-mouthed chinless man I had heard Whisper call Jerry came a step through it. He had a couple of guns. The more angular one of the blond kids who had been in the King Street joint looked over his shoulder.

Dinah Brand got up from the chesterfield, put her back to Thaler, and addressed me. Her voice was husky with rage.

'This is none of my doing. He came here by himself, said he was sorry for what he had said, and showed me how we could make a lot of coin by turning Noonan up for you. The whole thing was a plant, but I fell for it. Honest to Christ! He was to wait upstairs while I put it to you. I didn't know anything about the others. I didn't—'

Jerry's casual voice drawled:

'If I shoot a pin from under her, she'll sure sit down, and maybe shut up. O.K.?'

I couldn't see Whisper. The girl was between us. He said:

'Not now. Where's Dan?'

The angular blond youngster said:

'Up on the bathroom floor. I had to sap him.'

Dinah Brand turned around to face Thaler. Stocking seams made s's up the ample backs of her legs. She said:

'Max Thaler, you're a lousy little—'

He whispered, very deliberately:

'Shut up and get out of the way.'

She surprised me by doing both, and she kept quiet while he spoke to me:

'So you and Noonan are trying to paste his brother's death on me?'

'It doesn't need pasting. It's a natural.'

He curved his thin lips at me and said:

'You're as crooked as he is.'

I said:

'You know better. I played your side when he tried to frame you. This time he's got you copped to rights.'

Dinah Brand flared up again, waving her arms in the center of the room, storming:

'Get out of here, the whole lot of you. Why should I give a goddamn about your troubles? Get out.'

The blond kid who had sapped Rolff squeezed past Jerry and came grinning into the room. He caught one of the girl's flourished arms and bent it behind her.

She twisted toward him, socked him in the belly with her other fist. It was a very respectable wallop – man-size. It broke his grip on her arm, sent him back a couple of steps.

The kid gulped a wide mouthful of air, whisked a blackjack from his hip, and stepped in again. His grin was gone.

Jerry laughed what little chin he had out of sight.

Thaler whispered harshly: 'Lay off!'

The kid didn't hear him. He was snarling at the girl.

She watched him with a face hard as a silver dollar. She was standing with most of her weight on her left foot. I guessed blondy was going to stop a kick when he closed in.

The kid feinted a grab with his empty left hand, started the blackjack at her face.

Thaler whispered, 'Lay off,' again, and fired.

The bullet smacked blondy under the right eye, spun him around, and dropped him backwards into Dinah Brand's arms.

This looked like the time, if there was to be any.

In the excitement I had got my hand to my hip. Now I yanked the gun out and snapped a cap at Thaler, trying for his shoulder.

That was wrong. If I had tried for a bull's-eye I would have winged him. Chinless Jerry hadn't laughed himself blind. He beat me to the shot. His shot burnt my wrist, throwing me off the target. But, missing Thaler, my slug crumpled the red-faced man behind him.

Not knowing how badly my wrist was nicked, I switched the gun to my left hand.

Jerry had another try at me. The girl spoiled it by heaving the corpse at him. The dead yellow head banged into his knees. I jumped for him while he was off-balance.

The jump took me out of the path of Thaler's bullet. It also tumbled me and Jerry out into the hall, all tangled up together.

Jerry wasn't tough to handle, but I had to work quick. There was Thaler behind me. I socked Jerry twice, kicked him, butted him at least once, and was hunting for a place to bite when he went limp under me. I poked him again where his chin should have been – just to make sure he wasn't faking – and went away on hands and knees, down the hall a bit, out of line with the door.

I sat on my heels against the wall, held my gun level at Thaler's part of the premises, and waited. I couldn't hear anything for the moment except blood singing in my head.

Dinah Brand stepped out of the door I had tumbled through, looked at Jerry, then at me. She smiled with her tongue between her teeth, beckoned with a jerk of her head, and returned to the living room. I followed her cautiously.

Whisper stood in the center of the floor. His hands were empty and so was his face. Except for his vicious little mouth he looked like something displaying suits in a clothing store window.

Dan Rolff stood behind him, with a gun-muzzle tilted to the little gambler's left kidney. Rolff's face was mostly blood. The blond kid – now dead on the floor between Rolff and me – had sapped him plenty.

I grinned at Thaler and said. 'Well, this is nice,' before I saw that Rolff had another gun, centered on my chubby middle. That wasn't so nice. But my gun was reasonably level in my hand. I didn't have much worse than an even break.

Rolff said:

'Put down your pistol.'

I looked at Dinah, looked puzzled, I suppose. She shrugged and told me:

'It seems to be Dan's party.'

'Yeah? Somebody ought to tell him I don't like to play this way.'

Rolff repeated: 'Put down your pistol.'

I said disagreeably:

'I'm damned if I will. I've shed twenty pounds trying to nab this bird, and I can spare twenty more for the same purpose.'

Rolff said:

'I'm not interested in what is between you two, and I have no intention of giving either of you—'

Dinah Brand had wandered across the room. When she was behind Rolff, I interrupted his speech by telling her:

'If you upset him now you're sure of making two friends – Noonan and me. You can't trust Thaler any more, so there's no use helping him.'

She laughed and said:

'Talk money, darling.'

'Dinah!' Rolff protested. He was caught. She was behind him and she was strong enough to handle him. It wasn't likely that he would shoot her, and it wasn't likely that anything else would keep her from doing whatever she decided to do.

'A hundred dollars,' I bid.

'My God!' she exclaimed, 'I've actually got a cash offer out of you. But not enough.'

'Two hundred.'

'You're getting reckless. But I still can't hear you.'

'Try,' I said. 'It's worth that to me not to have to shoot Rolff's gun out of his hand, but no more than that.'

'You got a good start. Don't weaken. One more bid, anyway.'

'Two hundred dollars and ten cents and that's all.'

'You big bum,' she said, 'I won't do it.'

'Suit yourself.' I made a face at Thaler and cautioned him: 'When what happens happens be damned sure you keep still.'

Dinah cried:

'Wait! Are you really going to start something?'

'I'm going to take Thaler out with me, regardless.'

'Two hundred and a dime?'

'Yeah.'

'Dinah,' Rolff called without turning his face from me, 'you won't—'

But she laughed, came close to his back, and wound her strong arms around him, pulling his arms down, pinning them to his sides.

I shoved Thaler out of the way with my right arm, and kept my gun on him while I yanked Rolff's weapons out of his hands. Dinah turned the lunger loose.

He took two steps toward the dining room door, said wearily, 'There is no—' and collapsed on the floor.

Dinah ran to him. I pushed Thaler through the hall door, past the still sleeping Jerry, and to the alcove beneath the front stairs, where I had seen a phone.

I called Noonan, told him I had Thaler, and where.

'Mother of God!' he said. 'Don't kill him till I get there.'

# 14
# Max

The news of Whisper's capture spread quickly. When Noonan, the coppers he had brought along, and I took the gambler and the now conscious Jerry into the City Hall there were at least a hundred people standing around watching us.

All of them didn't look pleased. Noonan's coppers – a shabby lot at best – moved around with whitish strained faces. But Noonan was the most triumphant guy west of the Mississippi. Even the bad luck he had trying to third-degree Whisper couldn't spoil his happiness.

Whisper stood up under all they could give him. He would talk to his lawyer, he said, and to nobody else, and he stuck to it. And, as much as Noonan hated the gambler, here was a prisoner he didn't give the works, didn't turn over to the wrecking crew. Whisper had killed the chief's brother, and the chief hated his guts, but Whisper was still too much somebody in Poisonville to be roughed around.

Noonan finally got tired of playing with his prisoner, and sent him up – the prison was on the City Hall's top floor – to be stowed away. I lit another of the chief's cigars and read the detailed statement he had got from the woman in the hospital.

There was nothing in it that I hadn't learned from Dinah and MacSwain.

The chief wanted me to come out to his house for dinner, but I lied out of it, pretending that my wrist – now in a bandage – was bothering me. It was really little more than a burn.

While we were talking about it, a pair of plain-clothes men brought in the red-faced bird who had stopped the slug I had missed Whisper with. It had broken a rib for him, and he had taken a back-door sneak while the rest of us were busy. Noonan's men had picked him up in a doctor's office. The chief failed to get any information out of him, and sent him off to the hospital.

I got up and prepared to leave, saying:

'The Brand girl gave me the tip-off on this. That's why I asked you to keep her and Rolff out of it.'

The chief took hold of my left hand for the fifth or sixth time in the past couple of hours.

'If you want her taken care of, that's enough for me,' he assured me. 'But if she had a hand in turning that bastard up, you can tell her for me that any time she wants anything, all she's got to do is name it.'

I said I'd tell her that, and went over to my hotel, thinking about that neat white bed. But it was nearly eight o'clock, and my stomach needed attention. I went into the hotel dining room and had that fixed up.

Then a leather chair tempted me into stopping in the lobby while I burnt a cigar. That led to conversation with a traveling railroad auditor from Denver, who knew a man I knew in St Louis. Then there was a lot of shooting in the street.

We went to the door and decided that the shooting was in the vicinity of the City Hall. I shook the auditor and moved up that way.

I had done two-thirds of the distance when an automobile came down the street toward me, moving fast, leaking gun-fire from the rear.

I backed into an alley entrance and slid my gun loose. The car came abreast. An arc-light brightened two faces in the front of the car. The driver's meant nothing to me. The upper part of the other's was hidden by a pulled-down hat. The lower part was Whisper's.

Across the street was the entrance to another block of my alley, lighted at the far end. Between the light and me, somebody moved just as Whisper's car roared past. The somebody had dodged from behind one shadow that might have been an ash-can to another.

What made me forget Whisper was that the somebody's legs had a bowed look.

A load of coppers buzzed past, throwing lead at the first car.

I skipped across the street, into the section of alley that held a man who might have bowed legs.

If he was my man, it was a fair bet he wasn't armed. I played it that way, moving straight up the slimy middle of the alley, looking into shadows with eyes, ears and nose.

Three-quarters of a block of this, and a shadow broke away from another shadow – a man going pell-mell away from me.

'Stop!' I bawled, pounding my feet after him. 'Stop, or I'll plug you, MacSwain.'

He ran half a dozen strides farther and stopped, turning.

'Oh, it's you,' he said, as if it made any difference who took him back to the hoosegow.

'Yeah,' I confessed. 'What are all you people doing wandering around loose?'

'I don't know nothing about it. Somebody dynamited the floor out of the can. I dropped through the hole with the rest of them. There was some mugs standing off the bulls. I made the back-trotters with one bunch. Then we split, and I was figuring on cutting over and making the hills. I didn't have nothing to do with it. I just went along when she blew open.'

'Whisper was pinched this evening,' I told him.

'Hell! Then that's it. Noonan had ought to know he'd never keep that guy screwed up – not in this burg.'

We were standing still in the alley where MacSwain had stopped running.

'You know what he was pinched for?' I asked.

'Uh-huh, for killing Tim.'

'You know who killed Tim?'

'Huh? Sure, he did.'

'You did.'

'Huh? What's the matter? You simple?'

'There's a gun in my left hand,' I warned him.

'But look here – didn't he tell the broad that Whisper done it? What's the matter with you?'

'He didn't say *Whisper*. I've heard women call Thaler *Max*, but I've never heard a man here call him anything but *Whisper*. Tim didn't say *Max*. He said *MacS* – the first part of *MacSwain* – and died before he could finish it. Don't forget about the gun.'

'What would I have killed him for? He was after Whisper's—'

'I haven't got around to that yet,' I admitted, 'but let's see: You and your wife had busted up. Tim was a ladies' man, wasn't he? Maybe there's something there. I'll have to look it up. What started me thinking about you was that you never tried to get any more money out of the girl.'

'Cut it out,' he begged. 'You know there ain't any sense to it. What would I have hung around afterwards for? I'd have been out getting an alibi, like Whisper.'

'Why? You were a dick then. Close by was the spot for you – to see that everything went right – handle it yourself.'

'You know damned well it don't hang together, don't make sense. Cut it out, for God's sake.'

'I don't mind how goofy it is,' I said. 'It's something to put to Noonan when we get back. He's likely all broken up over Whisper's crush-out. This will take his mind off it.'

MacSwain got down on his knees in the muddy alley and cried:

'Oh, Christ, no! He'd croak me with his hands.'

'Get up and stop yelling,' I growled. 'Now will you give it to me straight?'

He whined: 'He'd croak me with his hands.'

'Suit yourself. If you won't talk, I will, to Noonan. If you'll come through to me, I'll do what I can for you.'

'What can you do?' he asked hopelessly, and started sniveling again. 'How do I know you'll try to do anything?'

I risked a little truth on him:

'You said you had a hunch what I'm up to here in Poisonville. Then you ought to know that it's my play to keep Noonan and Whisper split. Letting Noonan think Whisper killed Tim will keep them split. But if you don't want to play with me, come on, we'll play with Noonan.'

'You mean you won't tell him?' he asked eagerly. 'You promise?'

'I promise you nothing,' I said. 'Why should I? I've got you with your pants down. Talk to me or Noonan. And make up your mind quick. I'm not going to stand here all night.'

He made up his mind to talk to me.

'I don't know how much you know, but it was like you said, my wife fell for Tim. That's what put me on the tramp. You can ask anybody if I wasn't a good guy before that. I was this way: what she wanted I wanted her to have. Mostly what she wanted was tough on me. But I couldn't be any other way. We'd have been a damned sight better off if I could. So I let her move out and put in divorce papers, so she could marry him, thinking he meant to.

'Pretty soon I begin to hear he's chasing this Myrtle Jennison. I couldn't go that. I'd given him his chance with Helen, fair and square. Now he was giving her the air for this Myrtle. I wasn't going to stand for that. Helen wasn't no hanky-panky. It was accidental, though, running into him at the Lake that night.

When I saw him go down to them summer houses I went after him. That looked like a good quiet place to have it out.

'I guess we'd both had a little something to drink. Anyway, we had it hot and heavy. When it got too hot for him, he pulled the gun. He was yellow. I grabbed it, and in the tussle it went off. I swear to God I didn't shoot him except like that. It went off while the both of us had our hands on it. I beat it back in some bushes. But when I got in the bushes I could hear him moaning and talking. There was people coming – a girl running down from the hotel, that Myrtle Jennison.

'I wanted to go back and hear what Tim was saying, so I'd know where I stood, but I was leary of being the first one there. So I had to wait till the girl got to him, listening all the time to his squawking, but too far away to make it out. When she got to him, I ran over and got there just as he died trying to say my name.

'I didn't think about that being Whisper's name till she propositioned me with the suicide letter, the two hundred, and the rock. I'd just been stalling around, pretending to get the job lined up – being on the force then – and trying to find out where I stood. Then she makes the play and I know I'm sitting pretty. And that's the way it went till you started digging it up again.'

He slopped his feet up and down in the mud and added:

'Next week my wife got killed – an accident. Uh-huh, an accident. She drove the Ford square in front of No 6 where it comes down the long grade from Tanner and stopped it there.'

'Is Mock Lake in this county?' I asked.

'No, Boulder County.'

'That's out of Noonan's territory. Suppose I take you over there and hand you to the sheriff?'

'No. He's Senator Keefer's son-in-law – Tom Cook. I might as well be here. Noonan could get to me through Keefer.'

'If it happened the way you say, you've got at least an even chance of beating the rap in court.'

'They won't give me a chance. I'd have stood it if there'd been a chance in the world of getting an even break – but not with them.'

'We're going back to the Hall,' I said. 'Keep your mouth shut.'

Noonan was waddling up and down the floor, cursing the half a dozen bulls who stood around wishing they were somewhere else.

'Here's something I found roaming around,' I said, pushing MacSwain forward.

Noonan knocked the ex-detective down, kicked him, and told one of the coppers to take him away.

Somebody called Noonan on the phone. I slipped out without saying, 'Good-night,' and walked back to the hotel.

Off to the north some guns popped.

A group of three men passed me, shifty-eyed, walking pigeon-toed.

A little farther along, another man moved all the way over to the curb to give me plenty of room to pass. I didn't know him and didn't suppose he knew me.

A lone shot sounded not far away.

As I reached the hotel, a battered black touring car went down the street, hitting fifty at least, crammed to the curtains with men.

I grinned after it. Poisonville was beginning to boil out under the lid, and I felt so much like a native that even the memory of my very un-nice part in the boiling didn't keep me from getting twelve solid end-to-end hours of sleep.

# 15
# Cedar Hill Inn

Mickey Linehan used the telephone to wake me a little after noon.

'We're here,' he told me. 'Where's the reception committee?'

'Probably stopped to get a rope. Check your bags and come up to the hotel. Room 537. Don't advertise your visit.'

I was dressed when they arrived.

Mickey Linehan was a big slob with sagging shoulders and a shapeless body that seemed to be coming apart at all its joints. His ears stood out like red wings, and his round red face usually wore the meaningless smirk of a half-wit. He looked like a comedian and was.

Dick Foley was a boy-sized Canadian with a sharp irritable face. He wore high heels to increase his height, perfumed his handkerchiefs and saved all the words he could.

They were both good operatives.

'What did the Old Man tell you about the job?' I asked when we had settled into seats. The Old Man was the manager of the Continental's San Francisco branch. He was also known as Pontius Pilate, because he smiled pleasantly when he sent us out to be crucified on suicidal jobs. He was a gentle, polite, elderly person with no more warmth in him than a hangman's rope. The Agency wits said he could spit icicles in July.

'He didn't seem to know much what it was all about,' Mickey said, 'except that you had wired for help. He said he hadn't got any reports from you for a couple of days.'

'The chances are he'll wait a couple more. Know anything about this Personville?'

Dick shook his head. Mickey said:

'Only that I've heard parties call it Poisonville like they meant it.'

I told them what I knew and what I had done. The telephone bell interrupted my tale in the last quarter.

Dinah Brand's lazy voice:

'Hello! How's the wrist?'

'Only a burn. What do you think of the crush-out?'

'It's not my fault,' she said. 'I did my part. If Noonan couldn't hold him, that's just too bad. I'm coming downtown to buy a hat this afternoon. I thought I'd drop in and see you for a couple of minutes if you're going to be there.'

'What time?'

'Oh, around three.'

'Right, I'll expect you, and I'll have that two hundred and a dime I owe you.'

'Do,' she said. 'That's what I'm coming in for. Ta-ta.'

I went back to my seat and my story.

When I had finished, Mickey Linehan whistled and said:

'No wonder you're scared to send in any reports. The Old Man wouldn't do much if he knew what you've been up to, would he?'

'If it works out the way I want it to, I won't have to report all the distressing details,' I said. 'It's right enough for the Agency to have rules and regulations, but when you're out on a job you've got to do it the best way you can. And anybody that brings any ethics to Poisonville is going to get them all rusty. A report is no place for the dirty details, anyway, and I don't want you birds to send any writing back to San Francisco without letting me see it first.'

'What kind of crimes have you got for us to pull?' Mickey asked.

'I want you to take Pete the Finn. Dick will take Lew Yard. You'll have to play it the way I've been playing – do what you can when you can. I've an idea that the pair of them will try to make Noonan let Whisper alone. I don't know what he'll do. He's shifty as hell and he does want to even up his brother's killing.'

'After I take this Finnish gent,' Mickey said, 'what do I do with him? I don't want to brag about how dumb I am, but this job is plain as astronomy to me. I understand everything about it except what you have done and why, and what you're trying to do and how.'

'You can start off by shadowing him. I've got to have a wedge that can be put between Pete and Yard, Yard and Noonan, Pete and Noonan, Pete and Thaler, or Yard and Thaler. If we can smash things up enough – break the combination – they'll have their knives in each other's backs, doing our work for us. The break between Thaler and Noonan is a starter. But it'll sag on us if we don't help it along.

'I could buy more dope on the whole lot from Dinah Brand. But there's no use taking anybody into court, no matter what you've got on them. They own the courts, and, besides, the courts are too slow for us now. I've got myself tangled up in something and as soon as the Old Man smells it – and San Francisco isn't far enough away to fool his nose – he's going to be sitting on the wire, asking for explanations. I've got to have results to hide the details under. So evidence won't do. What we've got to have is dynamite.'

'What about our respected client, Mr Elihu Willsson?' Mickey asked. 'What are you planning to do with or to him?'

'Maybe ruin him, maybe club him into backing us up. I don't care which. You'd better stay at the Hotel Person, Mickey, and Dick can go to the National. Keep apart, and, if you want to keep me from being fired, burn the job up before the Old Man tumbles. Better write these down.'

I gave them names, descriptions, and addresses when I had them, of Elihu Willsson; Stanley Lewis, his secretary; Dinah Brand; Dan Rolff; Noonan; Max Thaler, alias Whisper; his right-hand man, the chinless Jerry; Mrs Donald Willsson; Lewis's daughter, who had been Donald Willsson's secretary; and Bill Quint, Dinah's radical ex-boy-friend.

'Now hop to it,' I said. 'And don't kid yourselves that there's any law in Poisonville except what you make for yourself.'

Mickey said I'd be surprised how many laws he could get along without. Dick said: 'So long,' and they departed.

After breakfast I went over to the City Hall.

Noonan's greenish eyes were bleary, as if they hadn't been sleeping, and his face had lost some of its color. He pumped my hand up and down as enthusiastically as ever, and the customary amount of cordiality was in his voice and manner.

'Any line on Whisper?' I asked when we had finished the glad-handing.

'I think I've got something.' He looked at the clock on the wall and then at his phone. 'I'm expecting word any minute. Sit down.'

'Who else got away?'

'Jerry Hooper and Tony Agosti are the only other ones still out. We picked up the rest. Jerry is Whisper's man-Friday, and the wop's one of his mob. He's the bozo that put the knife in Ike Bush the night of the fight.'

'Any more of Whisper's mob in?'

'No. We just had the three of them, except Buck Wallace, the fellow you potted. He's in the hospital.'

The chief looked at the wall clock again, and at his watch. It was exactly two o'clock. He turned to the phone. It rang. He grabbed it, said:

'Noonan talking . . . Yes . . . Yes . . . Yes . . . Right.'

He pushed the phone aside and played a tune on the row of pearl buttons on his desk. The office filled up with coppers.

'Cedar Hill Inn,' he said. 'You follow me out with your detail, Bates. Terry, shoot out Broadway and hit the dump from behind. Pick up the boys on traffic duty as you go along. It's likely we'll need everybody we can get. Duffy, take yours out Union Street and around by the old mine road. McGraw will hold headquarters down. Get hold of everybody you can and send them after us. Jump!'

He grabbed his hat and went after them, calling over his thick shoulder to me:

'Come on, man, this is the kill.'

I followed him down to the department garage, where the engines of half a dozen cars were roaring. The chief sat beside his driver. I sat in back with four detectives.

Men scrambled into the others cars. Machine-guns were unwrapped. Arm-loads of rifles and riot-guns were distributed, and packages of ammunition.

The chief's car got away first, off with a jump that hammered our teeth together. We missed the garage door by half an inch, chased a couple of pedestrians diagonally across the sidewalk, bounced off the curb into the roadway, missed a truck as narrowly as we had missed the door, and dashed out King Street with our siren wide open.

Panicky automobiles darted right and left, regardless of traffic rules, to let us through. It was a lot of fun.

I looked back, saw another police car following us, a third turning into Broadway. Noonan chewed a cold cigar and told the driver:

'Give her a bit more, Pat.'

Pat twisted us around a frightened woman's coupé, put us through a slot between street car and laundry wagon – a narrow slot that we couldn't have slipped through if our car hadn't been so smoothly enameled – and said:

'All right, but the brakes ain't no good.'

'That's nice,' the gray-mustached sleuth on my left said. He didn't sound sincere.

Out of the center of the city there wasn't much traffic to bother us, but the paving was rougher. It was a nice half-hour's ride, with everybody getting a chance to sit in everybody else's lap. The last ten minutes of it was over an uneven road that had hills enough to keep us from forgetting what Pat had said about the brakes.

We wound up at a gate topped by a shabby electric sign that had said *Cedar Hill Inn* before it lost its globes. The roadhouse, twenty feet behind the gate, was a squat wooden building painted a moldy green and chiefly surrounded by rubbish. Front door and windows were closed, blank.

We followed Noonan out of the car. The machine that had been trailing us came into sight around a bend in the road, slid to rest beside ours, and unloaded its cargo of men and weapons.

Noonan ordered this and that.

A trio of coppers went around each side of the building. Three others, including a machine-gunner, remained by the gate. The rest of us walked through tin cans, bottles, and ancient newspaper to the front of the house.

The gray-mustached detective who had sat beside me in the car carried a red ax. We stepped up on the porch.

Noise and fire came out under a window sill.

The gray-mustached detective fell down, hiding the ax under his corpse.

The rest of us ran away.

I ran with Noonan. We hid in the ditch on the Inn side of the road. It was deep enough, and banked high enough, to let us stand almost erect without being targets.

The chief was excited.

'What luck!' he said happily. 'He's here, by God, he's here!'

'That shot came from under the sill,' I said. 'Not a bad trick.'

'We'll spoil it, though,' he said cheerfully. 'We'll sieve the dump. Duffy ought to be pulling up on the other road by now, and Terry Shane won't be many minutes behind him. Hey, Donner!' he called to a man who was peeping around a boulder. 'Swing around back and tell Duffy and Shane to start closing in as soon as they come, letting fly with all they got. Where's Kimble?'

The peeper jerked a thumb toward a tree beyond him. We could see only the upper part of it from our ditch.

'Tell him to set up his mill and start grinding,' Noonan ordered. 'Low, across the front, ought to do it like cutting cheese.'

The peeper disappeared.

Noonan went up and down the ditch, risking his noodle over the top now and then for a look around, once in a while calling or gesturing to his men.

He came back, sat on his heels beside me, gave me a cigar, and lit one for himself.

'It'll do,' he said complacently. 'Whisper won't have a chance. He's done.'

The machine-gun by the tree fired, haltingly, experimentally, eight or ten shots. Noonan grinned and let a smoke ring float out of his mouth. The machine-gun settled down to business, grinding out metal like the busy little death factory it was. Noonan blew another smoke ring and said:

'That's exactly what'll do it.'

I agreed that it ought to. We leaned against the clay bank and smoked while, farther away, another machine-gun got going, and then a third. Irregularly, rifles, pistols, shot-guns joined in. Noonan nodded approvingly and said:

'Five minutes of that will let him know there's a hell.'

When the five minutes were up I suggested a look at the

remains. I gave him a boost up the bank and scrambled up after him.

The roadhouse was as bleak and empty-looking as before, but more battered. No shots came from it. Plenty were going into it.'

'What do you think?' Noonan asked.

'If there's a cellar there might be a mouse alive in it.'

'Well, we could finish him afterwards.'

He took a whistle out of his pocket and made a lot of noise. He waved his fat arms, and the gun-fire began dwindling. We had to wait for the word to go all the way around.

Then we crashed the door.

The first floor was ankle-deep with booze that was still gurgling from bullet holes in the stacked-up cases and barrels that filled most of the house.

Dizzy with the fumes of spilled hooch, we waded around until we had found four dead bodies and no live ones. The four were swarthy foreign-looking men in laborers' clothes. Two of them were practically shot to pieces.

Noonan said:

'Leave them here and get out.'

His voice was cheerful, but in a flashlight's glow his eyes showed white-ringed with fear.

We went out gladly, though I did hesitate long enough to pocket an unbroken bottle labeled *Dewar*.

A khaki-dressed copper was tumbling off a motorcycle at the gate. He yelled at us:

'The First National's been stuck up.'

Noonan cursed savagely, bawled:

'He's foxed us, damn him! Back to town, everybody.'

Everybody except us who had ridden with the chief beat it for the machines. Two of them took the dead detective with them.

Noonan looked at me out of his eye-corners and said:

'This is a tough one, no fooling.'

I said, 'Well,' shrugged, and sauntered over to his car, where the driver was sitting at the wheel. I stood with my back to the house, talking to Pat. I don't remember what we talked about. Presently Noonan and the other sleuths joined us.

Only a little flame showed through the open roadhouse door before we passed out of sight around the bend in the road.

# 16
# Exit Jerry

There was a mob around the First National Bank. We pushed through it to the door, where we found sour-faced McGraw.

'Was six of them, masked,' he reported to the chief as we went inside. 'They hit it about two-thirty. Five of them got away clean with the jack. The watchman here dropped one of them, Jerry Hooper. He's over on the bench, cold. We got the roads blocked, and I wired around, if it ain't too late. Last seen of them was when they made the turn into King Street, in a black Lincoln.'

We went over to look at the dead Jerry, lying on one of the lobby benches with a brown robe over him. The bullet had gone under his left shoulder blade.

The bank watchman, a harmless looking old duffer, pushed up his chest and told us about it:

'There wasn't no chance to do nothing at first. They were in 'fore anybody knew anything. And maybe they didn't work fast. Right down the line, scooping it up. No chance to do anything then. But I says to myself. "All righty, young fellows, you've got it all your own way now, but wait till you try to leave." '

'And I was as good as my word, you bet you. I runs right to

the door after them and cut loose with the old firearm. I got that fellow just as he was stepping into the car. I bet you I'd of got more of them if I'd of had more cartridges, because it's kind of hard shooting down like that, standing in the—'

Noonan stopped the monologue by patting the old duffer's back till his lungs were empty, telling him, 'That certainly is fine. That certainly is fine.'

McGraw pulled the robe up over the dead man again and growled:

'Nobody can identify anybody. But with Jerry on it, it's a cinch it was Whisper's caper.'

The chief nodded happily and said:

'I'll leave it in your hands, Mac. Going to poke around here, or going back to the Hall with me?' he asked me.

'Neither. I've got a date, and I want to get into dry shoes.'

Dinah Brand's little Marmon was standing in front of the hotel. I didn't see her. I went up to my room, leaving the door unlocked. I had got my hat and coat off when she came in without knocking.

'My God, you keep a boozy smelling room,' she said.

'It's my shoes. Noonan took me wading in rum.'

She crossed to the window, opened it, sat on the sill, and asked:

'What was that for?'

'He thought he was going to find your Max out in a dump called Cedar Hill Inn. So we went out there, shot the joint silly, murdered some dagoes, spilled gallons of liquor, and left the place burning.'

'Cedar Hill Inn? I thought it had been closed up for a year or more.'

'It looked it, but it was somebody's warehouse.'

'But you didn't find Max there?' she asked.

'While we were there he seems to have been knocking over Elihu's First National Bank.'

'I saw that,' she said. 'I had just come out of Bengren's, the store two doors away. I had just got in my car when I saw a big boy backing out of the bank, carrying a sack and a gun, with a black handkerchief over his face.'

'Was Max with them?'

'No, he wouldn't be. He'd send Jerry and the boys. That's what he has them for. Jerry was there. I knew him as soon as he got out of the car, in spite of the black handkerchief. They all had black ones. Four of them came out of the bank, running down to the car at the curb. Jerry and another fellow were in the car. When the four came across the sidewalk, Jerry jumped out and went to meet them. That's when the shooting started and Jerry dropped. The others jumped in the bus and lit out. How about that dough you owe me?'

I counted out ten twenty-dollar bills and a dime. She left the window to come for them.

'That's for pulling Dan off, so you could cop Max,' she said when she had stowed the money away in her bag. 'Now how about what I was to get for showing you where you could turn up the dope on his killing Tim Noonan?'

'You'll have to wait till he's indicted. How do I know the dope's any good?'

She frowned and asked:

'What do you do with all the money you don't spend?' Her face brightened. 'You know where Max is now?'

'No.'

'What's it worth to know?'

'Nothing.'

'I'll tell you for a hundred bucks.'

'I wouldn't want to take advantage of you that way.'

'I'll tell you for fifty bucks.'

I shook my head.

'Twenty-five.'

'I don't want him,' I said. 'I don't care where he is. Why don't you peddle the news to Noonan?'

'Yes, and try to collect. Do you only perfume yourself with booze, or is there any for drinking purposes?'

'Here's a bottle of so-called Dewar that I picked up at Cedar Hill this afternoon. There's a bottle of King George in my bag. What's your choice?'

She voted for King George. We had a drink apiece, straight, and I said:

'Sit down and play with it while I change clothes.'

When I came out of the bathroom twenty-five minutes later she was sitting at the secretary, smoking a cigarette and studying a memoranda book that had been in a side pocket of my gladstone bag.

'I guess theses are the expenses you've charged up on other cases,' she said without looking up. 'I'm damned if I can see why you can't be more liberal with me. Look, here's a six-hundred-dollar item marked *Inf.* That's information you bought from somebody, isn't it? And here's a hundred and fifty below it – *Top* – whatever that is. And here's another day when you spent nearly a thousand dollars.'

'They must be telephone numbers,' I said, taking the book from her. 'Where were you raised? Fanning my baggage!'

'I was raised in a convent,' she told me. 'I won the good behavior prize every year I was there. I thought little girls who put extra spoons of sugar in their chocolate went to hell for gluttony. I didn't even know there was such a thing as profanity until I was eighteen. The first time I heard any I damned near fainted.' She spit on the rug in front of her, tilted her chair back, put her crossed feet on my bed, and asked: 'What do you think of that?'

I pushed her feet off the bed and said:

'I was raised in a water-front saloon. Keep your saliva off my floor or I'll toss you out on your neck.'

'Let's have another drink first. Listen, what'll you give me for the inside story of how the boys didn't lose anything building the City Hall – the story that was in the papers I sold Donald Willsson?'

'That doesn't click with me. Try another.'

'How about why the first Mrs Lew Yard was sent to the insane asylum?'

'No.'

'King, our sheriff, eight thousand dollars in debt four years ago, now the owner of as nice a collection of downtown business blocks as you'd want to see. I can't give you all of it, but I can show you where to get it.'

'Keep trying,' I encouraged her.

'No. You don't want to buy anything. You're just hoping you'll pick up something for nothing. This isn't bad Scotch. Where'd you get it?'

'Brought it from San Francisco with me.'

'What's the idea of not wanting any of this information I'm offering? Think you can get it cheaper?'

'Information of that kind's not much good to me now. I've got to move quick. I need dynamite – something to blow them apart.'

She laughed and jumped up, her big eyes sparkling.

'I've got one of Lew Yard's cards. Suppose we sent the bottle of Dewar you opened to Pete with the card. Wouldn't he take it as a declaration of war? If Cedar Hill was a liquor cache, it was Pete's. Wouldn't the bottle and Lew's card make him think Noonan had knocked the place over under orders?'

I considered it and said:

'Too crude. It wouldn't fool him. Besides, I'd just as leave have Pete and Lew both against the chief at this stage.'

She pouted and said:

'You think you know everything. You're just hard to get along with. Take me out tonight? I've got a new outfit that'll knock them cockeyed.'

'Yeah.'

'Come up for me around eight.'

She patted my cheek with a warm hand, said 'Ta-ta,' and went out as the telephone bell began jingling.

*

'My chinch and Dick's are together at your client's joint,' Mickey Linehan reported over the wire. 'Mine's been generally busier than a hustler with two bunks, though I don't know what the score is yet. Anything new?'

I said there wasn't and went into conference with myself across the bed, trying to guess what would come of Noonan's attack on Cedar Hill Inn and Whisper's on the First National Bank. I would have given something for the ability to hear what was being said up at old Elihu's house by him, Pete the Finn, and Lew Yard. But I hadn't that ability, and I was never much good at guessing, so after half an hour I stopped tormenting my brain and took a nap.

It was nearly seven o'clock when I came out of the nap. I washed, dressed, loaded my pockets with a gun and a pint flask of Scotch, and went up to Dinah's.

# 17
# Reno

She took me into her living room, backed away from me, revolved, and asked me how I liked the new dress. I said I liked it. She explained that the color was rose beige and that the dinguses on the side were something or other, winding up:

'And you really think I look good in it?'

'You always look good,' I said. 'Lew Yard and Pete the Finn went calling on old Elihu this afternoon.'

She made a face at me and said:

'You don't give a damn about my dress. What did they do there?'

'A pow-wow, I suppose.'

She looked at me through her lashes and asked:

'Don't you really know where Max is?'

Then I did. There was no use admitting I hadn't known all along. I said:

'At Willsson's, probably, but I haven't been interested enough to make sure.'

'That's goofy of you. He's got reasons for not liking you and me. Take mama's advice and nail him quick, if you like living and like having mama live too.'

I laughed and said:

'You don't know the worst of it. Max didn't kill Noonan's brother. Tim didn't say *Max*. He tried to say *MacSwain*, and died before he could finish.'

She grabbed my shoulders and tried to shake my hundred and ninety pounds. She was almost strong enough to do it.

'God damn you!' Her breath was hot in my face. Her face was white as her teeth. Rouge stood out sharply like red labels pasted on her mouth and cheeks. 'If you've framed him and made me frame him, you've got to kill him – now.'

I don't like being manhandled, even by young women who look like something out of mythology when they're steamed up. I took her hands off my shoulders, and said:

'Stop bellyaching. You're still alive.'

'Yes, still. But I know Max better than you do. I know how much chance anybody that frames him has got of staying alive long. It would be bad enough if we had got him right, but—'

'Don't make so much fuss over it. I've framed my millions and nothing's happened to me. Get your hat and coat and we'll feed. You'll feel better then.'

'You're crazy if you think I'm going out. Not with that—'

'Stop it, sister. If he's that dangerous he's just as likely to get you here as anywhere. So what difference does it make?'

'It makes a— You know what you're going to do? You're going to stay here until Max is out of the way. It's your fault and you've got to look out for me. I haven't even got Dan. He's in the hospital.'

'I can't,' I said. 'I've got work to do. You're all burnt up over nothing. Max has probably forgotten all about you by now. Get your hat and coat. I'm starving.'

She put her face close to mine again, and her eyes looked as if they had found something horrible in mine.

'Oh, you're rotten!' she said. 'You don't give a damn what happens to me. You're using me as you use the others – that dynamite you wanted. I trusted you.'

'You're dynamite, all right, but the rest of it's kind of foolish. You look a lot better when you're happy. Your features are heavy. Anger makes them downright brutal. I'm starving, sister.'

'You'll eat here,' she said. 'You're not going to get me out after dark.'

She meant it. She swapped the rose beige dress for an apron, and took inventory of the ice box. There were potatoes, lettuce, canned soup and half a fruit cake. I went out and got a couple of steaks, rolls, asparagus, and tomatoes.

When I came back she was mixing gin, vermouth and orange bitters in a quart shaker, not leaving a lot a space for them to move around in.

'Did you see anything?' she asked.

I sneered at her in a friendly way. We carried the cocktails into the dining room and played bottoms-up while the meal cooked. The drinks cheered her a lot. By the time we sat down to the food she had almost forgotten her fright. She wasn't a very good cook, but we ate as if she were.

We put a couple of gin-gingerales in on top the dinner.

She decided she wanted to go places and do things. No lousy little runt could keep her cooped up, because she had been as square with him as anybody could be until he got nasty over nothing, and if he didn't like what she did he could go climb trees or jump in lakes, and we'd go out to the Silver Arrow where she had meant to take me, because she had promised Reno she'd show up at his party, and by God she would, and anybody who thought she wouldn't was crazy as a pet cuckoo, and what did I think of that?

'Who's Reno?' I asked while she tied herself tighter in the apron by pulling the strings the wrong way.

'Reno Starkey. You'll like him. He's a right guy. I promised him I'd show at his celebration and that's just what I'll do.'

'What's he celebrating?'

'What the hell's the matter with this lousy apron? He was sprung this afternoon.'

'Turn around and I'll unwind you. What was he in for? Stand still.'

'Blowing a safe six or seven months ago – Turlock's, the jeweler. Reno, Put Collings, Blackie Whalen, Hank O'Marra, and a little lame guy called Step-and-a-Half. They had plenty of cover – Lew Yard – but the jewelers' association dicks tied the job to them last week. So Noonan had to go through the motions. It doesn't mean anything. They got out on bail at five o'clock this afternoon, and that's the last anybody will ever hear about it. Reno's used to it. He was already out on bail for three other capers. Suppose you mix another little drink while I'm inserting myself in the dress.'

The Silver Arrow was half-way between Personville and Mock Lake.

'It's not a bad dump,' Dinah told me as her little Marmon carried us toward it. 'Polly De Voto is a good scout and anything she sells you is good, except maybe the bourbon. That always tastes a little bit like it had been drained off a corpse. You'll like her. You can get away with anything out here so long as you don't get noisy. She won't stand for noise. There it is. See the red and blue lights through the trees?'

We rode out of the woods into full view of the roadhouse, a very electric-lighted imitation castle set close to the road.

'What do you mean she won't stand for noise?' I asked, listening to the chorus of pistols singing *Bang-bang-bang*.

'Something up,' the girl muttered, stopping the car.

Two men dragging a woman between them ran out of the roadhouse's front door, ran away into the darkness. A man sprinted out a side door, away. The guns sang on. I didn't see any flashes.

Another man broke out and vanished around the back.

A man leaned far out a front second-story window, a black gun in his hand.

Dinah blew her breath out sharply.

From a hedge by the road, a flash of orange pointed briefly up at the man in the window. His gun flashed downward. He leaned farther out. No second flash came from the hedge.

The man in the window put a leg over the sill, bent, hung by his hands, dropped.

Our car jerked forward. Dinah's lower lip was between her teeth.

The man who had dropped from the window was gathering himself up on hands and knees.

Dinah put her face in front of mine and screamed:

'Reno!'

The man jumped up, his face to us. He made the road in three leaps, as we got to him.

Dinah had the little Marmon wide open before Reno's feet were on the running board beside me. I wrapped my arms around him, and damned near dislocated them holding him on. He made it as tough as he could for me by leaning out to try for a shot at the guns that were tossing lead all around us.

Then it was all over. We were out of range, sight and sound of the Silver Arrow, speeding away from Personville.

Reno turned around and did his own holding on. I took my arms in and found that all the joints still worked. Dinah was busy with the car.

Reno said:

'Thanks, kid. I needed pulling out.'

'That's all right,' she told him. 'So that's the kind of parties you throw?'

'We had guests that wasn't invited. You know the Tanner Road?'

'Yes.'

'Take it. It'll put us over to Mountain Boulevard, and we can get back to town that-a-way.'

The girl nodded, slowed up a little, and asked:

'Who were the uninvited guests?'

'Some plugs that don't know enough to leave me alone.'

'Do I know them?' she asked, too casually, as she turned the car into a narrower and rougher road.

'Let it alone, kid,' Reno said. 'Better get as much out of the heap as it's got.'

She prodded another fifteen miles an hour out of the Marmon. She had plenty to do now holding the car to the road, and Reno had plenty holding himself to the car. Neither of them made any more conversation until the road brought us into one that had more and better paving.

Then he asked:

'So you paid Whisper off?'

'Um-hmm.'

'They're saying you turned rat on him.'

'They would. What do you think?'

'Ditching him was all right. But throwing in with a dick and cracking the works to him is kind of sour. Damned sour, if you ask me.'

He looked at me while he said it. He was a man of thirty-four or -five, fairly tall, broad and heavy without fat. His eyes were large, brown, dull, and set far apart in a long, slightly sallow horse face. It was a humorless face, stolid, but somehow not unpleasant. I looked at him and said nothing.

The girl said: 'If that's the way you feel about it, you can—'

'Look out,' Reno grunted.

We had swung around a curve. A long black car was straight across the road ahead of us – a barricade.

Bullets flew around us. Reno and I threw bullets around while the girl made a polo pony of the little Marmon.

She shoved it over to the left of the road, let the left wheels ride the bank high, crossed the road again with Reno's and my weight on the inside, got the right bank under the left wheels just as our side of the car began to lift in spite of our weight, slid us down in the road with our backs to the enemy, and took us out of the neighborhood by the time we had emptied our guns.

A lot of people had done a lot of shooting, but so far as we could tell nobody's bullets had hurt anybody.

Reno, holding to the door with his elbows while he pushed another clip into his automatic, said:

'Nice work, kid. You handle the bus like you meant it.'

Dinah asked: 'Where now?'

'Far away first. Just follow the road. We'll have to figure it out. Looks like they got the burg closed up on us. Keep your dog on it.'

We put ten or twelve more miles between Personville and us. We passed a few cars, saw nothing to show we were being chased. A short bridge rumbled under us. Reno said:

'Take the right turn at the top of the hill.'

We took it, into a dirt road that wound between trees down the side of a rock-ridged hill. Ten miles an hour was fast going here. After five minutes of creeping along Reno ordered a halt. We heard nothing, saw nothing, during the half-hour we sat in darkness. Then Reno said:

'There's an empty shack a mile down the way. We'll camp there, huh? There's no sense trying to crash the city line again tonight.'

Dinah said she would prefer anything to being shot at again. I said it was all right with me, though I would rather have tried to find some path back to the city.

We followed the dirt track cautiously until our headlights settled on a small clapboard building that badly needed the paint it had never got.

'Is this it?' Dinah asked Reno.

'Uh-huh. Stay here till I look it over.'

He left us, appearing soon in the beam of our lights at the shack door. He fumbled with keys at the padlock, got it off, opened the door, and went in. Presently he came to the door and called:

'All right. Come in and make yourselves at home.'

Dinah cut off the engine and got out of the car.

'Is there a flashlight in the car?' I asked.

She said, 'Yes,' gave it to me, yawned, 'My God, I'm tired. I hope there's something to drink in the hole.'

I told her I had a flask of Scotch. The news cheered her up.

The shack was a one-room affair that held an army cot covered with brown blankets, a deal table with a deck of cards and some gummy poker chips on it, a brown iron stove, four chairs, an oil lamp, dishes, pots, pans and buckets, three shelves with canned food on them, a pile of firewood and a wheelbarrow.

Reno was lighting the lamp when we came in. He said:

'Not so tough. I'll hide the heap and then we'll be all set till daylight.'

Dinah went over to the cot, turned back the covers, and reported:

'Maybe there's things in it, but anyway it's not alive with them. Now let's have that drink.'

I unscrewed the flask and passed it to her while Reno went out to hide the car. When she had finished, I took a shot.

The purr of the Marmon's engine got fainter. I opened the door and looked out. Downhill, through trees and bushes, I could see broken chunks of white light going away. When I lost them for good I returned indoors and asked the girl:

'Have you ever had to walk home before?'

'What?'

'Reno's gone with the car.'

'The lousy tramp! Thank God he left us where there's a bed, anyway.'

'That'll get you nothing.'

'No?'

'No. Reno had a key to this dump. Ten to one the birds after him know about it. That's why he ditched us here. We're supposed to argue with them, hold them off his trail a while.'

She got up wearily from the cot, cursed Reno, me, all men from Adam on, and said disagreeably:

'You know everything. What do we do next?'

'We find a comfortable spot in the great open spaces, not too far away, and wait to see what happens.'

'I'm going to take the blankets.'

'Maybe one won't be missed, but you'll tip our mitts if you take more than that.'

'Damn your mitts,' she grumbled, but she took only one blanket.

I blew out the lamp, padlocked the door behind us, and with the help of the flashlight picked a way through the undergrowth.

On the hillside above we found a little hollow from which road and shack could be not too dimly seen through foliage thick enough to hide us unless we showed a light.

I spread that blanket there and we settled down.

The girl leaned against me and complained that the ground was damp, that she was cold in spite of her fur coat, that she had a cramp in her leg, and that she wanted a cigarette.

I gave her another drink from the flask. That bought me ten minutes of peace.

Then she said:

'I'm catching cold. By the time anybody comes, if they ever do, I'll be sneezing and coughing loud enough to be heard in the city.'

'Just once,' I told her. 'Then you'll be all strangled.'

'There's a mouse or something crawling under the blanket.'

'Probably only a snake.'

'Are you married?'

'Don't start that.'

'Then you are?'

'No.'

'I'll bet your wife's glad of it.'

I was trying to find a suitable come-back to that wise-crack when a distant light gleamed up the road. It disappeared as I sh-sh'd the girl.

'What is it?' she asked.

'A light. It's gone now. Our visitors have left their car and are finishing the trip afoot.'

A lot of time went by. The girl shivered with her cheek warm against mine. We heard footsteps, saw dark figures moving on the road and around the shack, without being sure whether we did or didn't.

A flashlight ended our doubt by putting a bright circle on the shack's door. A heavy voice said:

'We'll let the broad come out.'

There was a half-minute of silence while they waited for a reply from indoors. Then the same heavy voice asked: 'Coming?' Then more silence.

Gun-fire, a familiar sound tonight, broke the silence. Something hammered boards.

'Come on,' I whispered to the girl. 'We'll have a try at their car while they're making a racket.'

'Let them alone,' she said, pulling my arm down as I started up. 'I've had enough of it for one night. We're all right here.'

'Come on,' I insisted.

She said, 'I won't,' and she wouldn't, and presently, while we argued, it was too late. The boys below had kicked in the door, found the hut empty, and were bellowing for their car.

It came, took eight men aboard, and followed Reno's track downhill.

'We might as well move in again,' I said. 'It's not likely they'll be back this way tonight.'

'I hope to God there's some Scotch left in that flask,' she said as I helped her stand up.

# 18
# Painter Street

The shack's supply of canned goods didn't include any-thing that tempted us for breakfast. We made the meal of coffee cooked in very stale water from a galvanized pail.

A mile of walking brought us to a farmhouse where there was a boy who didn't mind earning a few dollars by driving us to town in the family Ford. He had a lot of questions, to which we gave him phoney answers or none. He set us down in front of a little restaurant in upper King Street, where we ate quantities of buckwheat cakes and bacon.

A taxi put us at Dinah's door a little before nine o'clock. I searched the place for her, from roof to cellar, and found no signs of visitors.

'When will you be back?' she asked as she followed me to the door.

'I'll try to pop in between now and midnight, if only for a few minutes. Where does Lew Yard live?'

'1622 Painter Street. Painter's three blocks over. 1622's four blocks up. What are you going to do there?' Before I could answer, she put her hands on my arm and begged: 'Get Max, will you? I'm afraid of him.'

'Maybe I'll sic Noonan on him a little later. It depends on how things work out.'

She called me a damned double-crossing something or other who didn't care what happened to her as long as his dirty work got done.

I went over to Painter Street. 1622 was a red brick house with a garage under the front porch.

A block up the street I found Dick Foley in a hired drive-yourself Buick. I got in beside him, asking:

'What's doing?'

'Spot two. Out three-thirty, office to Willsson's. Mickey. Five. Home. Busy. Kept plant. Off three, seven. Nothing yet.'

That was supposed to inform me that he had picked up Lew Yard at two the previous afternoon; had shadowed him to Willsson's at three-thirty, where Mickey had tailed Pete; had followed Yard away at five, to his residence; had seen people going in and out of the house, but had not shadowed any of them; had watched the house until three this morning, and had returned to the job at seven; and since then had seen nobody go in or out.

'You'll have to drop this and take a plant on Willsson's,' I said. 'I hear Whisper Thaler's holing-up there, and I'd like an eye kept on him till I make up my mind whether to turn him up for Noonan or not.'

Dick nodded and started the engine grinding. I got out and returned to the hotel.

There was a telegram from the Old Man:

SEND BY FIRST MAIL FULL EXPLANATION OF PRESENT OPERATION AND CIRCUMSTANCES UNDER WHICH YOU ACCEPTED IT WITH DAILY REPORTS TO DATE

I put the telegram in my pocket and hoped things would keep on breaking fast. To have sent him the dope he wanted at that time would have been the same as sending in my resignation.

I bent a fresh collar around my neck and trotted over to the City Hall.

'Hello,' Noonan greeted me. 'I was hoping you'd show up. Tried to get you at your hotel but they told me you hadn't been in.'

He wasn't looking well this morning, but under his gladhanding he seemed, for a change, genuinely glad to see me.

As I sat down one of his phones rang. He put the receiver to his ear, said 'Yes?' listened for a moment, said, 'You better go out there yourself, Mac,' and had to make two attempts to get the receiver back on its prong before he succeeded. His face had gone a little doughy, but his voice was almost normal as he told me:

'Lew Yard's been knocked off – shot coming down his front steps just now.'

'Any details?' I asked while I cursed myself for having pulled Dick Foley away from Painter Street an hour too soon. That was a tough break.

Noonan shook his head, staring at his lap.

'Shall we go out and look at the remains?' I suggested, getting up.

He neither got up nor looked up.

'No,' he said wearily to his lap. 'To tell the truth, I don't want to. I don't know as I could stand it just now. I'm getting sick of this killing. It's getting to me – on my nerves, I mean.'

I sat down again, considered his low spirits, and asked:

'Who do you guess killed him?'

'God knows,' he mumbled. 'Everybody's killing everybody. Where's it going to end?'

'Think Reno did it?'

Noonan winced, started to look up at me, changed his mind, and repeated:

'God knows.'

I went at him from another angle:

'Anybody knocked off in the battle at the Silver Arrow last night?'

'Only three.'

'Who were they?'

'A pair of Johnson-brothers named Blackie Whalen and Put Collings that only got out on bail around five yesterday, and Dutch Jake Wahl, a guerrilla.'

'What was it all about?'

'Just a roughhouse, I guess. It seems that Put and Blackie and the others that got out with them were celebrating with a lot of friends, and it wound up in smoke.'

'All of them Lew Yard's men?'

'I don't know anything about that,' he said.

I got up, said, 'Oh, all right,' and started for the door.

'Wait,' he called. 'Don't run off like that. I guess they were.'

I came back to my chair. Noonan watched the top of his desk. His face was gray, flabby, damp, like fresh putty.

'Whisper's staying at Willsson's,' I told him.

He jerked his head up. His eyes darkened. Then his mouth twitched, and he let his head sag again. His eyes faded.

'I can't go through with it,' he mumbled. 'I'm sick of this butchering. I can't stand any more of it.'

'Sick enough to give up the idea of evening the score for Tim's killing, if it'll make peace?' I asked.

'I am.'

'That's what started it,' I reminded him. 'If you're willing to call it off, it ought to be possible to stop it.'

He raised his face and looked at me with eyes that were like a dog's looking at a bone.

'The others ought to be as sick of it as you are,' I went on. 'Tell them how you feel about it. Have a get-together and make peace.'

'They'd think I was up to some kind of a trick,' he objected miserably.

'Have the meeting at Willsson's. Whisper's camping there. You'd be the one risking tricks going there. Are you afraid of that?'

He frowned and asked:

'Will you go with me?'

'If you want me.'

'Thanks,' he said. 'I–I'll try it.'

# 19
# The Peace Conference

All the other delegates to the peace conference were on hand when Noonan and I arrived at Willsson's home at the appointed time, nine o'clock that night. Everybody nodded to us, but the greetings didn't go any further than that.

Pete the Finn was the only one I hadn't met before. The bootlegger was a big-boned man of fifty with a completely bald head. His forehead was small, his jaws enormous – wide, heavy, bulging with muscle.

We sat around Willsson's library table.

Old Elihu sat at the head. The short-clipped hair on his round pink skull was like silver in the light. His round blue eyes were hard, domineering, under their bushy white brows. His mouth and chin were horizontal lines.

On his right Pete the Finn sat watching everybody with tiny black eyes that never moved. Reno Starkey sat next to the bootlegger. Reno's sallow horse face was as stolidly dull as his eyes.

Max Thaler was tilted back in a chair on Willsson's left. The little gambler's carefully pressed pants legs were carelessly crossed. A cigarette hung from one corner of his tight-lipped mouth.

I sat next to Thaler. Noonan sat on my other side.

Elihu Willsson opened the meeting.

He said things couldn't go on the way they were going. We were all sensible men, reasonable men, grown men who had seen enough of the world to know that a man couldn't have everything his own way, no matter who he was. Compromises were things everybody had to make sometimes. To get what he wanted, a man had to give other people what they wanted. He said he was sure that what we all most wanted now was to stop this insane killing. He said he was sure that everything could be frankly discussed and settled in an hour without turning Personville into a slaughterhouse.

It wasn't a bad oration.

When it was over there was a moment of silence. Thaler looked past me, at Noonan, as if he expected something of him. The rest of us followed his example, looking at the chief of police.

Noonan's face turned red and he spoke huskily:

'Whisper, I'll forget you killed Tim.' He stood up and held out a beefy paw. 'Here's my hand on it.'

Thaler's thin mouth curved into a vicious smile.

'Your bastard of a brother needed killing, but I didn't kill him,' he whispered coldly.

Red became purple in the chief's face.

I said loudly:

'Wait, Noonan. We're going at this wrong. We won't get anywhere unless everybody comes clean. Otherwise we'll all be worse off than before. MacSwain killed Tim, and you know it.'

He stared at me with dumbfounded eyes. He gaped. He couldn't understand what I had done to him.

I looked at the others, tried to look virtuous as hell, asked:

'That's settled, isn't it? Let's get the rest of the kicks squared.' I addressed Pete the Finn: 'How do you feel about yesterday's accident to your warehouse and the four men?'

'One hell of an accident,' he rumbled.

I explained:

'Noonan didn't know you were using the joint. He went there thinking it empty, just to clear the way for a job in town. Your men shot first, and then he really thought he had stumbled into Thaler's hideout. When he found he'd been stepping in your puddle he lost his head and touched the place off.'

Thaler was watching me with a hard small smile in eyes and mouth. Reno was all dull stolidity. Elihu Willsson was leaning toward me, his old eyes sharp and wary. I don't know what Noonan was doing. I couldn't afford to look at him. I was in a good spot if I played my hand right, and in a terrible one if I didn't.

'The men, they get paid for taking chances,' Pete the Finn said. 'For the other, twenty-five grand will make it right.'

Noonan spoke quickly, eagerly:

'All right, Pete, all right, I'll give it to you.'

I pushed my lips together to keep from laughing at the panic in his voice.

I could look at him safely now. He was licked, broken, willing to do anything to save his fat neck, or to try to. I looked at him.

He wouldn't look at me. He sat down and looked at nobody. He was busy trying to look as if he didn't expect to be carved apart before he got away from these wolves to whom I had handed him.

I went on with the work, turning to Elihu Willsson:

'Do you want to squawk about your bank being knocked over, or do you like it?'

Max Thaler touched my arm and suggested:

'We could tell better maybe who's entitled to beef if you'd give us what you've got first.'

I was glad to.

'Noonan wanted to nail you,' I told him, 'but he either got word, or expected to get word, from Yard and Willsson here to let you alone. So he thought if he had the bank looted and framed you for it, your backers would ditch you, and let him go after you right. Yard, I understand, was supposed to put his O.K. on all the capers in town. You'd be cutting into his territory, and gypping Willsson. That's how it would look. And that was supposed to make them hot enough that they'd help Noonan cop you. He didn't know you were here.

'Reno and his mob were in the can. Reno was Yard's pup, but he didn't mind crossing up his headman. He already had the idea that he was about ready to take the burg away from Lew.' I turned to Reno and asked: 'Isn't that it?'

He looked at me woodenly and said:

'You're telling it.'

I continued telling it:

'Noonan fakes a tip that you're at Cedar Hill, and takes all the coppers he can't trust out there with him, even cleaning the traffic detail out of Broadway, so Reno would have a clear road. McGraw and the bulls that are in on the play let Reno and his mob sneak out of the hoosegow, pull the job, and duck back in. Nice thing in alibis. Then they got sprung on bail a couple of hours later.

'It looks as if Lew Yard tumbled. He sent Dutch Jake Wahl and some other boys out to the Silver Arrow last night to teach Reno and his pals not to take things in their own hands like that. But Reno got away, and got back to the city. It was either him or Lew then. He made sure which it would be by being in front of Lew's house with a gun when Lew came out this morning. Reno seems to have had the right dope, because I notice that right now he's holding down a chair that would have been Lew Yard's if Lew hadn't been put on ice.'

Everybody was sitting very still, as if to call attention to how still they were sitting. Nobody could count on having any friends among those present. It was no time for careless motions on anybody's part.

If what I had said meant anything one way or the other to Reno he didn't show it.

Thaler whispered softly:

'Didn't you skip some of it?'

'You mean the part about Jerry?' I kept on being the life of the party. 'I was coming back to that. I don't know whether he got away from the can when you crushed out, and was caught later, or whether he didn't get away, or why. And I don't know how willingly he went along on the bank caper. But he did go along, and he was dropped and left in front of the bank because he was your right bower, and his being killed there would pin the trick to you. He was kept in the car till the get-away was on. Then he was pushed out, and was shot in the back. He was facing the bank, with his back to the car, when he got his.'

Thaler looked at Reno and whispered:

'Well?'

Reno looked with dull eyes at Thaler and asked calmly:

'What of it?'

Thaler stood up, said, 'Deal me out,' and walked to the door.

Pete the Finn stood up, leaning on the table with big bony hands, speaking from deep in his chest:

'Whisper.' And when Thaler had stopped and turned to face him: 'I'm telling you this. You, Whisper, and all of you. That damn gun-work is out. All of you understand it. You've got no brains to know what is best for yourselves. So I'll tell you. This busting the town open is no good for business. I won't have it any more. You be nice boys or I'll make you.

'I got one army of young fellows that know what to do on any end of a gun. I got to have them in my racket. If I got to use them on you I'll use them on you. You want to play with gunpowder and dynamite? I'll show you what playing is. You like to fight? I'll give you fighting. Mind what I tell you. That's all.'

Pete the Finn sat down.

Thaler looked thoughtful for a moment, and went away without saying or showing what he had thought.

His going made the others impatient. None wanted to

remain until anybody else had time to accumulate a few guns in the neighborhood.

In a very few minutes Elihu Willsson and I had the library to ourselves.

We sat and looked at one another.

Presently he said:

'How would you like to be chief of police?'

'No. I'm a rotten errand boy.'

'I don't mean with this bunch. After we've got rid of them.'

'And got another just like them.'

'Damn you,' he said, 'it wouldn't hurt to take a nicer tone to a man old enough to be your father.'

'Who curses me and hides behind his age.'

Anger brought a vein out blue in his forehead. Then he laughed.

'You're a nasty talking lad,' he said, 'but I can't say you haven't done what I paid you to do.'

'A swell lot of help I've got from you.'

'Did you need wet-nursing? I gave you the money and a free hand. That's what you asked for. What more did you want?'

'You old pirate,' I said, 'I blackmailed you into it, and you played against me all the way till now, when even you can see that they're hell-bent on gobbling each other up. Now you talk about what you did for me.'

'Old pirate,' he repeated. 'Son, if I hadn't been a pirate I'd still be working for the Anaconda for wages, and there'd be no Personville Mining Corporation. You're a damned little woolly lamb yourself, I suppose. I was had, son, where the hair was short. There were things I didn't like – worse things that I didn't know about until tonight – but I was caught and had to bide my time. Why since that Whisper Thaler has been here I've been a prisoner in my own home, a damned hostage!'

'Tough. Where do you stand now?' I demanded. 'Are you behind me?'

'If you win.'

I got up and said:

'I hope to Christ you get caught with them.'

He said:

'I reckon you do, but I won't.' He squinted his eyes merrily at me. 'I'm financing you. That shows I mean well, don't it? Don't be too hard on me, son, I'm kind of—'

I said, 'Go to hell,' and walked out.

# 20
# Laudanum

Dick Foley in his hired car was at the next corner. I had
him drive me over to within a block of Dinah Brand's
house, and walked the rest of the way.

'You look tired,' she said when I had followed her into the
living room. 'Been working?'

'Attending a peace conference out of which at least a dozen
killings ought to grow.'

The telephone rang. She answered it and called me.

Reno Starkey's voice:

'I thought maybe you'd like to hear about Noonan being shot
to hell and gone when he got out of his heap in front of his
house. You never saw anybody that was deader. Must have had
thirty pills pumped in him.'

'Thanks.'

Dinah's big blue eyes asked questions.

'First fruits of the peace conference, plucked by Whisper
Thaler,' I told her. 'Where's the gin?'

'Reno talking, wasn't it?'

'Yeah. He thought I'd like to hear about Poisonville being all
out of police chiefs.'

'You mean—?'

'Noonan went down tonight, according to Reno. Haven't you got any gin? Or do you like making me ask for it?'

'You know where it is. Been up to some of your cute tricks?'

I went back into the kitchen, opened the top of the refrigerator, and attacked the ice with an ice pick that had a six-inch awl-sharp blade set in a round blue and white handle. The girl stood in the doorway and asked questions. I didn't answer them while I put ice, gin, lemon juice and seltzer together in two glasses.

'What have you been doing?' she demanded as we carried our drinks into the dining room. 'You look ghastly.'

I put my glass on the table, sat down facing it, and complained:

'This damned burg's getting me. If I don't get away soon I'll be going blood-simple like the natives. There's been what? A dozen and a half murders since I've been here. Donald Willsson; Ike Bush; the four wops and the dick at Cedar Hill; Jerry; Lew Yard; Dutch Jake, Blackie Whalen and Put Collings at the Silver Arrow; Big Nick, the copper I potted; the blond kid Whisper dropped here; Yakima Shorty, old Elihu's prowler; and now Noonan. That's sixteen of them in less than a week, and more coming up.'

She frowned at me and said sharply:

'Don't look like that.'

I laughed and went on:

'I've arranged a killing or two in my time, when they were necessary. But this is the first time I've ever got the fever. It's this damned burg. You can't go straight here. I got myself tangled at the beginning. When old Elihu ran out on me there was nothing I could do but try to set the boys against each other. I had to swing the job the best way I could. How could I help it if the best way was bound to lead to a lot of killing? The job couldn't be handled any other way without Elihu's backing.'

'Well, if you couldn't help it, what's the use of making a lot of fuss over it? Drink your drink.'

I drank half of it and felt the urge to talk some more.

'Play with murder enough and it gets you one of two ways. It makes you sick, or you get to like it. It got Noonan the first way. He was green around the gills after Yard was knocked off, all the stomach gone out of him, willing to do anything to make peace. I took him in, suggested that he and the other survivors get together and patch up their differences.

'We had the meeting at Willsson's tonight. It was a nice party. Pretending I was trying to clear away everybody's misunderstandings by coming clean all around, I stripped Noonan naked and threw him to them – him and Reno. That broke up the meeting. Whisper declared himself out. Pete told everybody where they stood. He said battling was bad for his bootlegging racket, and anybody who started anything from then on could expect to have his booze guards turned loose on them. Whisper didn't look impressed. Neither did Reno.'

'They wouldn't be,' the girl said. 'What did you do to Noonan? I mean how did you strip him and Reno?'

'I told the others that he had known all along that MacSwain killed Tim. That was the only lie I told them. Then I told them about the bank stick-up being turned by Reno and the chief, with Jerry taken along and dropped on the premises to tie the job to Whisper. I knew that's the way it was if what you told me was right, about Jerry getting out of the car, starting toward the bank and being shot. The hole was in his back. Fitting in with that, McGraw said the last seen of the stick-up car was when it turned into King Street. The boys would be returning to the City Hall, to their jail alibi.'

'But didn't the bank watchman say he shot Jerry? That's the way it was in the papers.'

'He said so, but he'd say anything and believe it. He probably emptied his gun with his eyes shut, and anything that fell was his. Didn't you see Jerry drop?'

'Yes, I did, and he was facing the bank, but it was all too confused for me to see who shot him. There were a lot of men shooting, and—'

'Yeah. They'd see to that. I also advertised the fact – at least, it looks like a fact to me – that Reno plugged Lew Yard. This Reno is a tough egg, isn't he? Noonan went watery, but all they got out of Reno was a "What of it?" It was all nice and gentlemanly. They were evenly divided – Pete and Whisper against Noonan and Reno. But none of them could count on his partner backing him up if he made a play, and by the time the meeting was over the pairs had been split. Noonan was out of the count, and Reno and Whisper, against each other, had Pete against them. So everybody sat around and behaved and watched everybody else while I juggled death and destruction.

'Whisper was the first to leave, and he seems to have had time to collect some rods in front of Noonan's house by the time the chief reached home. The chief was shot down. If Pete the Finn meant what he said – and he has the look of a man who would – he'll be out after Whisper. Reno was as much to blame for Jerry's death as Noonan, so Whisper ought to be gunning for him. Knowing it, Reno will be out to get Whisper first, and that will set Pete on his trail. Besides that, Reno will likely have his hands full standing off those of the late Lew Yard's underlings who don't fancy Reno as boss. All in all it's one swell dish.'

Dinah Brand reached across the table and patted my hand. Her eyes were uneasy. She said:

'It's not your fault, darling. You said yourself that there was nothing else you could do. Finish your drink and we'll have another.'

'There was plenty else I could do,' I contradicted her. 'Old Elihu ran out on me at first simply because these birds had too much on him for him to risk a break unless he was sure they could be wiped out. He couldn't see how I could do it, so he played with them. He's not exactly their brand of cut-throat, and, besides, he thinks the city is his personal property, and he doesn't like the way they've taken it away from him.

'I could have gone to him this afternoon and showed him that I had them ruined. He'd have listened to reason. He'd have come over to my side, have given me the support I needed to swing the play legally. I could have done that. But it's easier to have them killed off, easier and surer, and, now that I'm feeling this way, more satisfying. I don't know how I'm going to come out with the Agency. The Old Man will boil me in oil if he ever finds out what I've been doing. It's this damned town. Poison-ville is right. It's poisoned me.

'Look. I sat at Willsson's table tonight and played them like you'd play trout, and got just as much fun out of it. I looked at Noonan and knew he hadn't a chance in a thousand of living another day because of what I had done to him, and I laughed, and felt warm and happy inside. That's not me. I've got hard skin all over what's left of my soul, and after twenty years of messing around with crime I can look at any sort of a murder without seeing anything in it but my bread and butter, the day's work. But this getting a rear out of planning deaths is not natural to me. It's what this place has done to me.'

She smiled too softly and spoke too indulgently:

'You exaggerate so, honey. They deserve all they get. I wish you wouldn't look like that. You make me feel creepy.'

I grinned, picked up the glasses, and went out to the kitchen for more gin. When I came back she frowned at me over anxious dark eyes and asked:

'Now what did you bring the ice pick in for?'

'To show you how my mind's running. A couple of days ago, if I thought about it at all, it was as a good tool to pry off chunks of ice.' I ran a finger down its half-foot of round steel blade to the needle point. 'Not a bad thing to pin a man to his clothes with. That's the way I'm begging, on the level. I can't even see a mechanical cigar lighter without thinking of filling one with nitroglycerine for somebody you don't like. There's a piece of copper wire lying in the gutter in front of your house – thin, soft, and just long enough to go around a neck with two ends to hold on. I had one hell of a time to keep from picking it up and stuffing it in my pocket, just in case—'

'You're crazy.'

'I know it. That's what I've been telling you. I'm going blood-simple.'

'Well, I don't like it. Put that thing back in the kitchen and sit down and be sensible.'

I obeyed two-thirds of the order.

'The trouble with you is,' she scolded me, 'your nerves are shot. You've been through too much excitement in the last few days. Keep it up and you're going to have the heebie-jeebies for fair, a nervous breakdown.'

I held up a hand with spread fingers. It was steady enough.

She looked at it and said:

'That doesn't mean anything. It's inside you. Why don't you sneak off for a couple of days' rest? You've got things here so they'll run themselves. Let's go down to Salt Lake. It'll do you good.'

'Can't, sister. Somebody's got to stay here to count the dead. Besides, the whole program is based on the present combination of people and events. Our going out of town would change that, and the chances are the whole thing would have to be gone over again.'

'Nobody would have to know you were gone, and I've got nothing to do with it.'

'Since when?'

She leaned forward, made her eyes small, and asked:

'Now what are you getting at?'

'Nothing. Just wondering how you got to be a disinterested bystander all of a sudden. Forgotten that Donald Willsson was killed because of you, starting the whole thing? Forgotten that it was the dope you gave me on Whisper that kept the job from petering out in the middle?'

'You know just as well as I do that none of that was my fault,' she said indignantly. 'And it's all past, anyway. You're just bringing it up because you're in a rotten humor and want to argue.'

'It wasn't past last night, when you were scared stiff Whisper was going to kill you.'

'Will you stop talking about killing!'

'Young Albury once told me Bill Quint had threatened to kill you,' I said.

'Stop it.'

'You seem to have a gift for stirring up murderous notions in your boy friends. There's Albury waiting trial for killing Willsson. There's Whisper who's got you shivering in corners. Even I haven't escaped your influence. Look at the way I've turned. And I've always had a private notion that Dan Rolff's going to have a try at you some day.'

'Dan! You're crazy. Why, I—'

'Yeah. He was a lunger and down and out, and you took him in. You gave him a home and all the laudanum he wants. You use him for errand boy, you slap his face in front of me, and slap him around in front of others. He's in love with you. One of these mornings you're going to wake up and find he's whittled your neck away.'

She shivered, got up and laughed.

'I'm glad one of us knows what you're talking about, if you do,' she said as she carried out empty glasses through the kitchen door.

I lit a cigarette and wondered why I felt the way I did, wondered if I were getting psychic, wondered whether there was anything in this presentiment business or whether my nerves were just ragged.

'The next best thing for you to do if you won't go away,' the girl advised me when she returned with full glasses, 'is to get plastered and forget everything for a few hours. I put a double slug of gin in yours. You need it.'

'It's not me,' I said, wondering why I was saying it, but somehow enjoying it. 'It's you. Every time I mention killing, you jump on me. You're a woman. You think if nothing's said about it, maybe none of the God only knows how many people in town who might want to will kill you. That's silly. Nothing we say or don't say is going to make Whisper, for instance—'

'Please, please stop! I am silly. I am afraid of the words. I'm afraid of him. I— Oh, why didn't you put him out of the way when I asked you?'

'Sorry,' I said, meaning it.

'Do you think he—?'

'I don't know,' I told her, 'and I reckon you're right. There's no use talking about it. The thing to do is drink, though there doesn't seem to be much body to this gin.'

'That's you, not the gin. Do you want an honest to God rear?'

'I'd drink nitroglycerine tonight.'

'That's just about what you're going to get,' she promised me.

She rattled bottles in the kitchen and brought me in a glass of what looked like the stuff we had been drinking. I sniffed at it and said:

'Some of Dan's laudanum, huh? He still in the hospital?'

'Yes. I think his skull is fractured. There's your kick, mister, if that's what you want.'

I put the doped gin down my throat. Presently I felt more comfortable. Time went by as we drank and talked in a world that was rosy, cheerful, and full of fellowship and peace on earth.

Dinah stuck to gin. I tried that for a while too, and then had another gin and laudanum.

For a while after that I played a game, trying to hold my eyes open as if I were awake, even though I couldn't see anything out of them. When the trick wouldn't fool her any more I gave it up.

The last thing I remembered was her helping me onto the living room chesterfield.

# 21
# The Seventeenth Murder

I dreamed I was sitting on a bench, in Baltimore, facing the tumbling fountain in Harlem Park, beside a woman who wore a veil. I had come there with her. She was somebody I knew well. But I had suddenly forgotten who she was. I couldn't see her face because of the long black veil.

I thought that if I said something to her I would recognize her voice when she answered. But I was very embarrassed and was a long time finding anything to say. Finally I asked her if she knew a man named Carroll T. Harris.

She answered me, but the roar and swish of the tumbling fountain smothered her voice, and I could hear nothing.

Fire engines went out Edmondson Avenue. She left me to run after them. As she ran she cried, 'Fire! Fire!' I recognized her voice then and knew who she was, and knew she was someone important to me. I ran after her, but it was too late. She and the fire engines were gone.

I walked streets hunting for her, half the streets in the United States, Gay Street and Mount Royal Avenue in Baltimore, Colfax Avenue in Denver, Aetna Road and St Clair Avenue in Cleveland, McKinney Avenue in Dallas, Lemartine and Cornell and Amory Streets in Boston, Berry Boulevard in Louisville,

Lexington Avenue in New York, until I came to Victoria Street in Jacksonville, where I heard her voice again, though I still could not see her.

I walked more streets, listening to her voice. She was calling a name, not mine, one strange to me, but no matter how fast I walked or in what direction, I could get no nearer her voice. It was the same distance from me in the street that runs past the Federal Building in El Paso as in Detroit's Grand Circus Park. Then the voice stopped.

Tired and discouraged, I went into the lobby of the hotel that faces the railroad station in Rocky Mount, North Carolina, to rest. While I sat there a train came in. She got off it and came into the lobby, over to me, and began kissing me. I was very uncomfortable because everybody stood around looking at us and laughing.

That dream ended there.

I dreamed I was in a strange city hunting for a man I hated. I had an open knife in my pocket and meant to kill him with it when I found him. It was Sunday morning. Church bells were ringing, crowds of people were in the streets, going to and from church. I walked almost as far as in the first dream, but always in this same strange city.

Then the man I was after yelled at me, and I saw him. He was a small brown man who wore an immense sombrero. He was standing on the steps of a tall building on the far side of a wide plaza, laughing at me. Between us, the plaza was crowded with people, packed shoulder to shoulder.

Keeping one hand on the open knife in my pocket, I ran toward the little brown man, running on the heads and shoulders of the people in the plaza. The heads and shoulders were of unequal heights and not evenly spaced. I slipped and floundered over them.

The little brown man stood on the steps and laughed until I had almost reached him. Then he ran into the tall building. I chased him up miles of spiral stairway, always just an inch more than a hand's reach behind him. We came to the roof. He ran straight across to the edge and jumped just as one of my hands touched him.

His shoulder slid out of my fingers. My hand knocked his sombrero off, and closed on his head. It was a smooth hard round head no larger than a large egg. My fingers went all the way around it. Squeezing his head in one hand – and realized that I had gone off the edge of the roof with him. We dropped giddily down toward the millions of upturned faces in the plaza, miles down.

I opened my eyes in the dull light of morning sun filtered through drawn blinds.

I was lying face down on the dining room floor, my head resting on my left forearm. My right arm was stretched straight out. My right hand held the round blue and white handle of Dinah Brand's ice pick. The pick's six-inch needle-sharp blade was buried in Dinah Brand's left breast.

She was lying on her back, dead. Her long muscular legs were stretched out toward the kitchen door. There was a run down the front of her right stocking.

Slowly, gently, as if afraid of awakening her, I let go the ice pick, drew in my arm, and got up.

My eyes burned. My throat and mouth were hot, woolly. I went into the kitchen, found a bottle of gin, tilted it to my mouth, and kept it there until I had to breathe. The kitchen clock said seven-forty-one.

With the gin in me I returned to the dining room, switched on the lights, and looked at the dead girl.

Not much blood was in sight: a spot the size of a silver dollar around the hole the ice pick made in her blue silk dress. There was a bruise on her right cheek, just under the cheek bone. Another bruise, finger-made, was on her right wrist. Her hands were empty. I moved her enough to see that nothing was under her.

I examined the room. So far as I could tell, nothing had been changed in it. I went back to the kitchen and found no recognizable changes there.

The spring lock on the back door was fastened, and had no marks to show it had been monkeyed with. I went to the front door and failed to find any marks on it. I went through the house from top to bottom, and learned nothing. The windows were all right. The girl's jewelry, on her dressing table (except the two diamond rings on her hands) and four hundred odd dollars in her handbag, on a bedroom chair, were undisturbed.

In the dining room again, I knelt beside the dead girl and used my handkerchief to wipe the ice pick handle clean of any prints my fingers had left on it. I did the same to glasses, bottles, doors, light buttons, and the pieces of furniture I had touched, or was likely to have touched.

Then I washed my hands, examined my clothes for blood, made sure I was leaving none of my property behind, and went to the front door. I opened it, wiped the inner knob, closed it behind me, wiped the outer knob, and went away.

From a drug store in upper Broadway I telephoned Dick Foley and asked him to come over to my hotel. He arrived a few minutes after I got there.

'Dinah Brand was killed in her house last night or early this morning,' I told him. 'Stabbed with an ice pick. The police don't know it yet. I've told you enough about her for you to know that there are any number of people who might have had reason for killing her. There are three I want looked up first – Whisper, Dan Rolff and Bill Quint, the radical fellow. You've got their descriptions. Rolff is in the hospital with a dented skull. I don't know which hospital. Try the City first. Get hold of Mickey Linehan – he's still camped on Pete the Finn's trail – and have him let Pete rest while he gives you a hand on this. Find out where those three birds were last night. And time means something.'

The little Canadian op had been watching me curiously while I talked. Now he started to say something, changed his mind, grunted, 'Righto,' and departed.

I went out to look for Reno Starkey. After an hour of searching I located him, by telephone, in a Ronney Street rooming house.

'By yourself?' he asked when I had said I wanted to see him.

'Yeah.'

He said I could come out, and told me how to get there. I took a taxi. It was a dingy two-story house near the edge of town.

A couple of men loitered in front of a grocer's on the corner above. Another pair sat on the low wooden steps of the house down at the next corner. None of the four was conspicuously refined in appearance.

When I rang the bell two men opened the door. They weren't so mild looking either.

I was taken upstairs to a front room where Reno, collarless and in shirt-sleeves and vest, sat tilted back in a chair with his feet on the window sill.

He nodded his sallow horse face and said:

'Pull a chair over.'

The men who had brought me up went away, closing the door. I sat down and said:

'I want an alibi. Dinah Brand was killed last night after I left her. There's no chance of my being copped for it, but with Noonan dead I don't know how I'm hitched up with the department. I don't want to give them any openings to even try to hang anything on me. If I've got to I can prove where I was last night, but you can save me a lot of trouble if you will.'

Reno looked at me with dull eyes and asked:

'Why pick on me?'

'You phoned me there last night. You're the only person who knows I was there the first part of the night. I'd have to fix it with you even if I got the alibi somewhere else, wouldn't I?'

He asked:

'You didn't croak her, did you?'

I said, 'No,' casually.

He stared out the window a little while before he spoke. He asked:

'What made you think I'd give you the lift? Do I owe you anything for what you done to me at Willsson's last night?'

I said:

'I didn't hurt you any. The news was half-out anyhow. Whisper knew enough to guess the rest. I only gave you a show-down. What do you care? You can take care of yourself.'

'I aim to try,' he agreed. 'All right. You was at the Tanner House in Tanner. That's a little burg twenty-thirty miles up the hill. You went up there after you left Willsson's and stayed till morning. A guy named Ricker that hangs around Murry's with a hire heap drove you up and back. You ought to know what you was doing up there. Give me your sig and I'll have it put on the register.'

'Thanks,' I said as I unscrewed my fountain pen.

'Don't say them. I'm doing this because I need all the friends I can get. When the time comes that you sit in with me and Whisper and Pete, I don't expect the sour end of it.'

'You won't get it,' I promised. 'Who's going to be chief of police?'

'McGraw's acting chief. He'll likely cinch it.'

'How'll he play?'

'With the Finn. Rough stuff will hurt his shop just like it does Pete's. It'll have to be hurt some. I'd be a swell mutt to sit still while a guy like Whisper is on the loose. It's me or him. Think he croaked the broad?'

'He had reason enough,' I said as I gave him the slip of paper on which I had written my name. 'She double-crossed him, sold him out, plenty.'

'You and her was kind of thick, wasn't you?' he asked.

I let the question alone, lighting a cigarette. Reno waited a while and then said:

'You better hunt up Ricker and let him get a look at you so's he'll know how to describe you if he's asked.'

A long-legged youngster of twenty-two or so with a thin freckled face around reckless eyes opened the door and came into the room. Reno introduced him to me as Hank O'Marra. I stood up to shake his hand, and then asked Reno:

'Can I reach you here if I need to?'

'Know Peak Murry?'

'I've met him, and I know his joint.'

'Anything you give him will get to me,' he said. 'We're getting out of here. It's not so good. That Tanner lay is all set.'

'Right. Thanks.' I went out of the house.

# 22
# The Ice Pick

D owntown, I went first to police headquarters. McGraw was holding down the chief's desk. His blond-lashed eyes looked suspiciously at me, and the lines in his leathery face were even deeper and sourer than usual.

'When'd you see Dinah Brand last?' he asked without any preliminaries, not even a nod. His voice rasped disagreeably through his bony nose.

'Ten-forty last night, or thereabout,' I said. 'Why?'

'Where?'

'Her house.'

'How long were you there?'

'Ten minutes, maybe fifteen.'

'Why?'

'Why what?'

'Why didn't you stay any longer than that?'

'What,' I asked, sitting down in the chair he hadn't offered me, 'makes it any of your business?'

He glared at me while he filled his lungs so he could yell, 'Murder!' in my face.

I laughed and said:

'You don't think she had anything to do with Noonan's killing?'

I wanted a cigarette, but cigarettes were too well known as first aids to the nervous for me to take a chance on one just then.

McGraw was trying to look through my eyes. I let him look, having all sorts of confidence in my belief that, like a lot of people, I looked most honest when I was lying. Presently he gave up the eye-study and asked:

'Why not?'

That was weak enough. I said, 'All right, why not?' indifferently, offered him a cigarette, and took one myself. Then I added: 'My guess is that Whisper did it.'

'Was he there?' For once McGraw cheated his nose, snapping the words off his teeth.

'Was he where?'

'At Brand's?'

'No,' I said, wrinkling my forehead. 'Why should he be – if he was off killing Noonan?'

'Damn Noonan!' the acting chief exclaimed irritably. 'What do you keep dragging him in for?'

I tried to look at him as if I thought him crazy.

He said:

'Dinah Brand was murdered last night.'

I said: 'Yeah?'

'Now will you answer my questions?'

'Of course. I was at Willsson's with Noonan and the others. After I left there, around ten-thirty, I dropped in at her house to tell her I had to go up to Tanner. I had a halfway date with her. I stayed there about ten minutes, long enough to have a drink. There was nobody else there, unless they were hiding. When was she killed? And how?'

McGraw told me he had sent a pair of his dicks – Shepp and Vanaman – to see the girl that morning, to see how much help she could and would give the department in copping Whisper for Noonan's murder. The dicks got to her house at nine-thirty.

The front door was ajar. Nobody answered their ringing. They went in and found the girl lying on her back in the dining room, dead, with a stab wound in her left breast.

The doctor who examined the body said she had been killed with a slender, round, pointed blade about six inches in length, at about three o'clock in the morning. Bureaus, closets, trunks, and so on, had apparently been skilfully and thoroughly ransacked. There was no money in the girl's handbag, or elsewhere in the house. The jewel case on her dressing table was empty. Two diamond rings were on her fingers.

The police hadn't found the weapon with which she had been stabbed. The fingerprint experts hadn't turned up anything they could use. Neither doors nor windows seemed to have been forced. The kitchen showed that the girl had been drinking with a guest or guests.

'Six inches, round, slim, pointed,' I repeated the weapon's description. 'That sounds like her ice pick.'

McGraw reached for the phone and told somebody to send Shepp and Vanaman in. Shepp was a stoop-shouldered tall man whose wide mouth had a grimly honest look that probably came from bad teeth. The other detective was short, stocky, with purplish veins in his nose and hardly any neck.

McGraw introduced us and asked them about the ice pick. They had not seen it, were positive it hadn't been there. They wouldn't have overlooked an article of its sort.

'Was it there last night?' McGraw asked me.

'I stood beside her while she chipped off pieces of ice with it.'

I described it. McGraw told the dicks to search her house again, and then to try to find the pick in the vicinity of the house.

'You knew her,' he said when Shepp and Vanaman had gone. 'What's your slant on it?'

'Too new for me to have one,' I dodged the question. 'Give me an hour or two to think it over. What do you think?'

He fell back into sourness, growling, 'How the hell do I know?'

But the fact that he let me go away without asking me any more questions told me he had already made up his mind that Whisper had killed the girl.

I wondered if the little gambler had done it, or if this was another of the wrong raps that Poisonville police chiefs liked to hang on him. It didn't seem to make much difference now. It was a cinch he had – personally or by deputy – put Noonan out, and they could only hang him once.

There were a lot of men in the corridor when I left McGraw. Some of these men were quite young – just kids – quite a few were foreigners, and most of them were every bit as tough looking as any men should be.

Near the street door I met Donner, one of the coppers who had been on the Cedar Hill expedition.

'Hello,' I greeted him. 'What's the mob? Emptying the can to make room for more?'

'Them's our new specials,' he told me, speaking as if he didn't think much of them. 'We're going to have a augmented force.'

'Congratulations,' I said and went on out.

In his pool room I found Peak Murry sitting at a desk behind the cigar counter talking to three men. I sat down on the other side of the room and watched two kids knock balls around. In a few minutes the lanky proprietor came over to me.

'If you see Reno some time,' I told him, 'you might let him know that Pete the Finn's having his mob sworn in as special coppers.'

'I might,' Murry agreed.

Mickey Linehan was sitting in the lobby when I got back to my hotel. He followed me up to my room, and reported:

'Your Dan Rolff pulled a sneak from the hospital somewhere

after midnight last night. The croakers are kind of steamed up about it. Seems they were figuring on pulling a lot of little pieces of bone out of his brain this morning. But him and his duds were gone. We haven't got a line on Whisper yet. Dick's out now trying to place Bill Quint. What's what on this girl's carving? Dick tells me you got it before the coppers.'

'It—'

The telephone bell rang.

A man's voice, carefully oratorical, spoke my name with a question mark after it.

I said: 'Yeah.'

The voice said:

'This is Mr Charles Proctor Dawn speaking. I think you will find it well worth your while to appear at my offices at your earliest convenience.'

'Will I? Who are you?'

'Mr Charles Proctor Dawn, attorney-at-law. My suite is in the Rutledge Block, 310 Green Street. I think you will find it well—'

'Mind telling me part of what it's about?' I asked.

'There are affairs best not discussed over the telephone. I think you will find—'

'All right,' I interrupted him again. 'I'll be around to see you this afternoon if I get a chance.'

'You will find it very, very advisable,' he assured me.

I hung up on that.

Mickey said:

'You were going to give me the what's what on the Brand slaughter.'

I said:

'I wasn't. I started to say it oughtn't to be hard to trace Rolff – running around with a fractured skull and probably a lot of bandages. Suppose you try it. Give Hurricane Street a play first.'

Mickey grinned all the way across his comedian's red face,

said, 'Don't tell me anything that's going on – I'm only working with you,' picked up his hat, and left me.

I spread myself on the bed, smoked cigarettes end to end, and thought about last night – my frame of mind, my passing out, my dreams, and the situation into which I woke. The thinking was unpleasant enough to make me glad when it was interrupted.

Fingernails scratched the outside of my door. I opened the door.

The man who stood there was a stranger to me. He was young, thin, and gaudily dressed. He had heavy eyebrows and a small mustache that were coal-black against a very pale, nervous, but not timid, face.

'I'm Ted Wright,' he said, holding out a hand as if I were glad to meet him. 'I guess you've heard Whisper talk about me.'

I gave him my hand, let him in, closed the door, and asked:

'You're a friend of Whisper's?'

'You bet.' He held up two thin fingers pressed tightly together. 'Just like that, me and him.'

I didn't say anything. He looked around the room, smiled nervously, crossed to the open bathroom door, peeped in, came back to me, rubbed his lips with his tongue, and made his proposition:

'I'll knock him off for you for a half a grand.'

'Whisper?'

'Yep, and it's dirt cheap.'

'Why do I want him killed?' I asked.

'He un-womaned you, didn't he?'

'Yeah?'

'You ain't that dumb.'

A notion stirred in my noodle. To give it time to crawl around I said: 'Sit down. This needs talking over.'

'It don't need nothing,' he said, looking at me sharply, not moving toward either chair. 'You either want him knocked off or you don't.'

173

'Then I don't.'

He said something I didn't catch, down in his throat, and turned to the door. I got between him and it. He stopped, his eyes fidgeting.

I said:

'So Whisper's dead?'

He stepped back and put a hand behind him. I poked his jaw, leaning my hundred and ninety pounds on the poke.

He got his legs crossed and went down.

I pulled him up by the wrists, yanked his face close to mine, and growled:

'Come through. What's the racket?'

'I ain't done nothing to you.'

'Let me catch you. Who got Whisper?'

'I don't know nothing a—'

I let go of one of his wrists, slapped his face with my open hand, caught his wrist again, and tried my luck at crunching both of them while I repeated:

'Who got Whisper?'

'Dan Rolff,' he whined. 'He walked up to him and stuck him with the same skewer Whisper had used on the twist. That's right.'

'How do you know it was the one Whisper killed the girl with?'

'Dan said so.'

'What did Whisper say?'

'Nothing. He looked funny as hell, standing there with the butt of the sticker sticking out his side. Then he flashes the rod and puts two pills in Dan just like one, and the both of them go down together, cracking heads, Dan's all bloody through the bandages.'

'And then what?'

'Then nothing. I roll them over, and they're a pair of stiffs. Every word I'm telling you is gospel.'

'Who else was there?'

'Nobody else. Whisper was hiding out, with only me to go between him and the mob. He killed Noonan himself, and he didn't want to have to trust nobody for a couple of days, till he could see what was what, excepting me.'

'So you, being a smart boy, thought you could run around to his enemies and pick up a little dough for killing him after he was dead?'

'I was clean, and this won't be no place for Whisper's pals when the word gets out that he's croaked,' Wright whined. 'I had to raise a get-away stake.'

'How'd you make out so far?'

'I got a century from Pete and a century and a half from Peak Murry – for Reno – with more promised from both when I turn the trick.' The whine changed into boasting as he talked. 'I bet you I could get McGraw to come across too, and I thought you'd kick in with something.'

'They must be high in the air to toss dough at a woozy racket like that.'

'I don't know,' he said superiorly. 'It ain't such a lousy one at that.' He became humble again. 'Give me a chance, chief. Don't gum it on me. I'll give you fifty bucks now and a split of whatever I get from McGraw if you'll keep your clam shut till I can put it over and grab a rattler.'

'Nobody but you knows where Whisper is?'

'Nobody else, except Dan, that's as dead as he is.'

'Where are they?'

'The old Redman warehouse down on Porter Street. In the back, upstairs, Whisper had a room fixed up with a bed, stove, and some grub. Give me a chance. Fifty bucks now and a cut on the rest.'

I let go of his arm and said:

'I don't want the dough, but go ahead. I'll lay off for a couple of hours. That ought to be long enough.'

'Thanks, chief. Thanks, thanks,' and he hurried away from me.

I put on my coat and hat, went out, found Green Street and the Rutledge Block. It was a wooden building a long while past any prime it might ever have had. Mr Charles Proctor Dawn's establishment was on the second floor. There was no elevator. I climbed a worn and rickety flight of wooden steps.

The lawyer had two rooms, both dingy, smelly, and poorly lighted. I waited in the outer one while a clerk who went well with the rooms carried my name in to the lawyer. Half a minute later the clerk opened the door and beckoned me in.

Mr Charles Proctor Dawn was a little fat man of fifty-something. He had prying triangular eyes of a very light color, a short fleshy nose, and a fleshier mouth whose greediness was only partly hidden between a ragged gray mustache and a ragged gray Vandyke beard. His clothes were dark and unclean looking without actually being dirty.

He didn't get up from his desk, and throughout my visit he kept his right hand on the edge of a desk drawer that was some six inches open.

He said:

'Ah, my dear sir, I am extremely gratified to find that you had the good judgment to recognize the value of my counsel.'

His voice was even more oratorical than it had been over the wire.

I didn't say anything.

Nodding his whiskers as if my not saying anything was another exhibition of good judgment, he continued:

'I may say, in all justice, that you will find it the invariable part of sound judgment to follow the dictates of my counsel in all cases. I may say this, my dear sir, without false modesty, appreciating with both fitting humility and a deep sense of true and lasting values, my responsibilities as well as my prerogatives as a – and why should I stoop to conceal the fact that there are those who feel justified in preferring to substitute the definite article for the indefinite? – recognized and accepted leader of the bar in this thriving state.'

He knew a lot of sentences like those, and he didn't mind using them on me. Finally he got along to:

'Thus, that conduct which in a minor practitioner might seem irregular, becomes, when he who exercises it occupies such indisputable prominence in his community – and, I might say, not merely the immediate community – as serves to place him above fear of reproach, simply that greater ethic which scorns the pettier conventionalities when confronted with an opportunity to serve mankind through one of its individual representatives. Therefore, my dear sir, I have not hesitated to brush aside scornfully all trivial considerations of accepted precedent, to summon you, to say to you frankly and candidly, my dear sir, that your interests will best be served by and through retaining me as your legal representative.'

I asked:

'What'll it cost?'

'That,' he said loftily, 'is of but secondary importance. However, it is a detail which has its deserved place in our relationship, and must be not overlooked or neglected. We shall say, a thousand dollars now. Later, no doubt—'

He ruffled his whiskers and didn't finish the sentence.

I said I hadn't, of course, that much money on me.

'Naturally, my dear sir. Naturally. But that is of not the least importance in any degree. None whatever. Any time will do for that, any time up to ten o'clock tomorrow morning.'

'At ten tomorrow,' I agreed. 'Now I'd like to know why I'm supposed to need legal representatives.'

He made an indignant face.

'My dear sir, this is no matter for jesting, of that I assure you.'

I explained that I hadn't been joking, that I really was puzzled.

He cleared his throat, frowned more or less importantly, said:

'It may well be, my dear sir, that you do not fully comprehend the peril that surrounds you, but it is indubitably preposterous that you should expect me to suppose that you are without any inkling of the difficulties – the legal difficulties, my dear sir – with which you are about to be confronted, growing, as they do, out of occurrences that took place at no more remote time than last night, my dear sir, last night. However, there is no time to go into that now. I have a pressing appointment with Judge Leffner. On the morrow I shall be glad to go more thoroughly into each least ramification of the situation – and I assure you they are many – with you. I shall expect you at ten tomorrow morning.'

I promised to be there, and went out. I spent the evening in my room, drinking unpleasant whiskey, thinking unpleasant thoughts, and waiting for reports that didn't come from Mickey and Dick. I went to sleep at midnight.

# 23
# Mr Charles Proctor Dawn

I was half dressed the next morning when Dick Foley came in. He reported, in his word-saving manner, that Bill Quint had checked out of the Miners' Hotel at noon the previous day, leaving no forwarding address.

A train left Personville for Ogden at twelve-thirty-five. Dick had wired the Continental's Salt Lake branch to send a man up to Ogden to try to trace Quint.

'We can't pass up any leads,' I said, 'but I don't think Quint's the man we want. She gave him the air long ago. If he had meant to do anything about it he would have done it before this. My guess is that when he heard she had been killed he decided to duck, being a discarded lover who had threatened her.'

Dick nodded and said:

'Gun-play out the road last night. Hijacking. Four trucks of hooch nailed, burned.'

That sounded like Reno Starkey's answer to the news that the big bootlegger's mob had been sworn in as special coppers.

Mickey Linehan arrived by the time I had finished dressing.

'Dan Rolff was at the house, all right,' he reported. 'The Greek grocer on the corner saw him come out around nine yesterday morning. He went down the street wobbling and talking to himself. The Greek thought he was drunk.'

'How come the Greek didn't tell the police? Or did he?'

'Wasn't asked. A swell department this burg's got. What do we do: find him for them and turn him in with the job all tacked up?'

'McGraw has decided Whisper killed her,' I said, 'and he's not bothering himself with any leads that don't lead that way. Unless he came back later for the ice pick, Rolff didn't turn the trick. She was killed at three in the morning. Rolff wasn't there at eight-thirty, and the pick was still sticking in her. It was—'

Dick Foley came over to stand in front of me and ask:

'How do you know?'

I didn't like the way he looked or the way he spoke. I said:

'You know because I'm telling you.'

Dick didn't say anything. Mickey grinned his half-wit's grin and asked:

'Where do we go from here? Let's get this thing polished off.'

'I've got a date for ten,' I told them. 'Hang around the hotel till I get back. Whisper and Rolff are probably dead – so we won't have to hunt for them.' I scowled at Dick and said: 'I was told that. I didn't kill either of them.'

The little Canadian nodded without lowering his eyes from mine.

I ate breakfast alone, and then set out for the lawyer's office.

Turning off King Street, I saw Hank O'Marra's freckled face in an automobile that was going up Green Street. He was sitting beside a man I didn't know. The long-legged youngster waved an arm at me and stopped the car. I went over to him.

He said:

'Reno wants to see you.'

'Where will I find him?'

'Jump in.'

'I can't go now,' I said. 'Probably not till afternoon.'

'See Peak when you're ready.'

I said I would. O'Marra and his companion drove on up Green Street. I walked half a block south to the Rutledge Block.

With a foot on the first of the rickety steps that led up to the lawyer's floor, I stopped to look at something.

It was barely visible back in a dim corner of the first floor. It was a shoe. It was lying in a position that empty shoes don't lie in.

I took my foot off the step and went toward the shoe. Now I could see an ankle and the cuff of a black pants-leg above the shoe-top.

That prepared me for what I found.

I found Mr Charles Proctor Dawn huddled among two brooms, a mop and a bucket, in a little alcove formed by the back of the stairs and a corner of the wall. His Vandyke beard was red with blood from a cut that ran diagonally across his forehead. His head was twisted sidewise and backward at an angle that could only be managed with a broken neck.

I quoted Noonan's 'What's got to be done has got to be done' to myself, and, gingerly pulling one side of the dead man's coat out of the way, emptied his inside coat pocket, transferring a black book and a sheaf of papers to my own pocket. In two of his other pockets I found nothing I wanted. The rest of his pockets couldn't be got at without moving him, and I didn't care to do that.

Five minutes later I was back in the hotel, going in through a side door, to avoid Dick and Mickey in the lobby, and walking up to the mezzanine to take an elevator.

In my room I sat down and examined my loot.

I took the book first, a small imitation-leather memoranda book of the sort that sells for not much money in any stationery store. It held some fragmentary notes that meant nothing to me, and thirty-some names and addresses that meant as little, with one exception:

That was interesting because, first, a young man named Robert Albury was in prison, having confessed that he shot and killed Donald Willsson in a fit of jealousy aroused by Willsson's supposed success with Dinah Brand; and, second, Dinah Brand had lived, and had been murdered, at 1232 Hurricane Street, across the street from 1229A.

I did not find my name in the book.

I put the book aside and began unfolding and reading the papers I had taken with it. Here too I had to wade through a lot that didn't mean anything to find something that did.

This find was a group of four letters held together by a rubber band.

The letters were in slitted envelopes that had postmarks dated a week apart, on the average. The latest was a little more than six months old. The letters were addressed to Dinah Brand. The first – that is, the earliest – wasn't so bad, for a love letter. The second was a bit goofier. The third and fourth were swell examples of how silly an ardent and unsuccessful wooer can be, especially if he's getting on in years. The four letters were signed by Elihu Willsson.

I had not found anything to tell me definitely why Mr Charles Proctor Dawn had thought he could blackmail me out of a thousand dollars, but I had found plenty to think about. I encouraged my brain with two Fatimas, and then went downstairs.

'Go out and see what you can raise on a lawyer named Charles Proctor Dawn,' I told Mickey. 'He's got offices in Green Street. Stay away from them. Don't put in a lot of time on him. I just want a rough line quick.'

I told Dick to give me a five-minute start and then follow me out to the neighborhood of 1229A Hurricane Street.

*

1299A was the upper flat in a two-story building almost dir-
ectly opposite Dinah's house. 1229 was divided into two flats,
with a private entrance for each. I rang the bell at the one I
wanted.

The door was opened by a thin girl of eighteen or nineteen
with dark eyes set close together in a shiny yellowish face under
short-cut brown hair that looked damp.

She opened the door, made a choked, frightened sound in
her throat, and backed away from me, holding both hands to
her mouth.

'Miss Helen Albury?' I asked.

She shook her head violently from side to side. There was no
truthfulness in it. Her eyes were crazy.

I said:

'I'd like to come in and talk to you a few minutes,' going in as
I spoke, closing the door behind me.

She didn't say anything. She went up the steps in front of me,
her head twisted around so she could watch me with her scary
eyes.

We went into a scantily furnished living room. Dinah's house
could be seen from its windows.

The girl stood in the center of the floor, her hands still to her
mouth.

I wasted time and words trying to convince her that I was
harmless. It was no good. Everything I said seemed to increase
her panic. It was a damned nuisance. I quit trying, and got
down to business.

'You are Robert Albury's sister?' I asked.

No reply, nothing but the senseless look of utter fear.

I said:

'After he was arrested for killing Donald Willsson you took
this flat so you could watch her. What for?'

Not a word from her. I had to supply my own answer:

'Revenge. You blamed Dinah Brand for your brother's
trouble. You watched for your chance. It came the night before

last. You sneaked into her house, found her drunk, stabbed her with the ice pick you found there.'

She didn't say anything. I hadn't succeeded in jolting the blankness out of her frightened face. I said:

'Dawn helped you, engineered it for you. He wanted Elihu Willsson's letters. Who was the man he sent to get them, the man who did the actual killing? Who was he?'

That got me nothing. No change in her expression, or lack of expression. No word. I thought I would like to spank her. I said:

'I've given you your chance to talk. I'm willing to listen to your side of the story. But suit yourself.'

She suited herself by keeping quiet, I gave it up. I was afraid of her, afraid she would do something even crazier than her silence if I pressed her further. I went out of the flat not sure that she had understood a single word I had said.

At the corner I told Dick Foley:

'There's a girl in there, Helen Albury, eighteen, five six, skinny, not more than a hundred, if that, eyes close together, brown, yellow skin, brown short hair, straight, got on a gray suit now. Tail her. If she cuts up on you throw her in the can. Be careful – she's crazy as a bedbug.'

I set out for Peak Murry's dump, to locate Reno and see what he wanted. Half a block from my destination I stepped into an office building doorway to look the situation over.

A police patrol wagon stood in front of Murry's. Men were being led, dragged, carried, from pool room to wagon. The leaders, draggers, and carriers, did not look like regular coppers. They were, I supposed, Pete the Finn's crew, now special officers. Pete, with McGraw's help, apparently was making good his threat to give Whisper and Reno all the war they wanted.

While I watched, an ambulance arrived, was loaded, and drove away. I was too far away to recognize anybody or any bodies. When the height of the excitement seemed past I circled a couple of blocks and returned to my hotel.

Mickey Linehan was there with information about Mr Charles Proctor Dawn.

'He's the guy that the joke was wrote about: "Is he a criminal lawyer?" "Yes, very." This fellow Albury that you nailed, some of his family hired this bird Dawn to defend him. Albury wouldn't have anything to do with him when Dawn came to see him. This three-named shyster nearly went over himself last year, on a blackmail rap, something to do with a person named Hill, but squirmed out of it. Got some property out on Libert Street, wherever that is. Want me to keep digging?'

'That'll do. We'll stick around till we hear from Dick.'

Mickey yawned and said that was all right with him, never being one that had to run around a lot to keep his blood circulating, and asked if I knew we were getting nationally famous.

I asked him what he meant by that.

'I just ran into Tommy Robins,' he said. 'The Consolidated Press sent him here to cover the doings. He tells me some of the other press associations and a big-city paper or two are sending in special correspondents, beginning to play our troubles up.'

I was making one of my favorite complaints – that newspapers were good for nothing except to hash things up so nobody could unhash them – when I heard a boy chanting my name. For a dime he told me I was wanted on the phone.

Dick Foley:

'She showed right away. To 310 Green Street. Full of coppers. Mouthpiece named Dawn killed. Police took her to the Hall.'

'She still there?'

'Yes, in the chief's office.'

'Stick, and get anything you pick up to me quick.'

I went back to Mickey Linehan and gave him my room key and instructions:

'Camp in my room. Take anything that comes for me and

pass it on. I'll be at the Shannon around the corner, registered as J. W. Clark. Tell Dick and nobody.'

Mickey asked, 'What the hell?' got no answer, and moved his loose-jointed bulk toward the elevators.

# 24
# Wanted

I went around to the Shannon Hotel, registered my alias, paid my day's rent, and was taken to room 321.

An hour passed before the phone rang.

Dick Foley said he was coming up to see me.

He arrived within five minutes. His thin worried face was not friendly. Neither was his voice. He said:

'Warrants out for you. Murder. Two counts – Brand and Dawn. I phoned. Mickey said he'd stick. Told me you were here. Police got him. Grilling him now.'

'Yeah, I expected that.'

'So did I,' he said sharply.

I said, making myself drawl the words:

'You think I killed them, don't you, Dick?'

'If you didn't, it's a good time to say so.'

'Going to put the finger on me?' I asked.

He pulled his lips back over his teeth. His face changed from tan to buff.

I said:

'Go back to San Francisco, Dick. I've got enough to do without having to watch you.'

He put his hat on very carefully and very carefully closed the door behind him when he went out.

At four o'clock, I had some lunch, cigarettes, and an *Evening Herald* sent up to me.

Dinah Brand's murder, and the newer murder of Charles Proctor Dawn, divided the front page of the *Herald*, with Helen Albury connecting them.

Helen Albury was, I read, Robert Albury's sister, and she was, in spite of his confession, thoroughly convinced that her brother was not guilty of murder, but the victim of a plot. She had retained Charles Proctor Dawn to defend him. (I could guess that the late Charles Proctor had hunted her up, and not she him.) The brother refused to have Dawn or any other lawyer, but the girl (properly encouraged by Dawn, no doubt) had not given up the fight.

Finding a vacant flat across the street of Dinah Brand's house, Helen Albury had rented it, and had installed herself therein with a pair of field glasses and one idea – to prove that Dinah and her associates were guilty of Donald Willsson's murder.

I, it seems, was one of the 'associates.' The *Herald* called me 'a man supposed to be a private detective from San Francisco, who has been in the city for several days, apparently on intimate terms with Max ("Whisper") Thaler, Daniel Rolff, Oliver ("Reno") Starkey, and Dinah Brand.' We were the plotters who had framed Robert Albury.

The night that Dinah had been killed, Helen Albury, peeping through her window, had seen things that were, according to the *Herald*, extremely significant when considered in connection with the subsequent finding of Dinah's dead body. As soon as the girl heard of the murder, she took her important knowledge to Charles Proctor Dawn. He, the police learned from his clerks, immediately sent for me, and had been closeted with me that afternoon. He had later told his clerks that I was to return the next – this – morning at ten. This morning I had not appeared to keep my appointment. At twenty-five minutes past ten, the janitor of the Rutledge Block had found Charles Proctor Dawn's body in a corner behind the staircase, murdered. It was believed that valuable papers had been taken from the dead man's pockets.

At the very moment that the janitor was finding the dead lawyer, I, it seems, was in Helen Albury's flat, having forced an entrance, and was threatening her. After she succeeded in throwing me out, she hurried to Dawn's offices, arriving while the police were there, telling them her story. Police sent to my hotel had not found me there, but in my room they had found one Michael Linehan, who also represented himself to be a San Francisco private detective. Michael Linehan was still being questioned by the police. Whisper, Reno, Rolff and I were being hunted by the police, charged with murder. Important developments were expected.

Page two held an interesting half-column. Detectives Shepp and Vanaman, the discoverers of Dinah Brand's body, had mysteriously vanished. Foul play on the part of us 'associates' was feared.

There was nothing in the paper about last night's hijacking, nothing about the raid on Peak Murry's joint.

I went out after dark. I wanted to get in touch with Reno.

From a drug store I phoned Peak Murry's pool room.

'Is Peak there?' I asked.

'This is Peak,' said a voice that didn't sound anything at all like his. 'Who's talking?'

I said disgustedly, 'This is Lillian Gish,' hung up the receiver, and removed myself from the neighborhood.

I gave up the idea of finding Reno and decided to go calling on my client, old Elihu, and try to blackjack him into good behavior with the love letters he had written Dinah Brand, and which I had stolen from Dawn's remains.

I walked, keeping to the darker side of the darkest streets. It was a fairly long walk for a man who sneers at exercise. By the time I reached Willsson's block I was in bad enough humor to be in good shape for the sort of interviews he and I usually had. But I wasn't to see him for a little while yet.

I was two pavements from my destination when somebody S-s-s-s-s'd at me.

I probably didn't jump twenty feet.

' 'S all right,' a voice whispered.

It was dark there. Peeping out under my bush – I was on my hands and knees in somebody's front yard – I could make out the form of a man crouching close to a hedge, on my side of it.

My gun was in my hand now. There was no special reason why I shouldn't take his word for it that it was all right.

I got up off my knees and went to him. When I got close enough I recognized him as one of the men who had let me into the Ronney Street house the day before.

I sat on my heels beside him and asked:

'Where'll I find Reno? Hank O'Marra said he wanted to see me.'

'He does that. Know where Kid McLeod's place is at?'

'No.'

'It's on Martin Street above King, corner the alley. Ask for the Kid. Go back that-away three blocks, and then down. You can't miss it.'

I said I'd try not to, and left him crouching behind his hedge, watching my client's place, waiting, I guessed, for a shot at Pete the Finn, Whisper, or any of Reno's other un-friends who might happen to call on old Elihu.

Following directions, I came to a soft drink and rummy establishment with red and yellow paint all over it. Inside I asked for Kid McLeod. I was taken into a back room, where a fat man with a dirty collar, a lot of gold teeth, and only one ear, admitted he was McLeod.

'Reno sent for me,' I said, 'Where'll I find him?'

'And who does that make you?' he asked.

I told him who I was. He went out without saying anything. I waited ten minutes. He brought a boy back with him, a kid of fifteen or so with a vacant expression on a pimply red face.

'Go with Sonny,' Kid McLeod told me.

I followed the boy out a side door, down two blocks of back street, across a sandy lot, through a ragged gate, and up to the back door of a frame house.

The boy knocked on the door and was asked who he was.

'Sonny, with a guy the Kid sent,' he replied.

The door was opened by long-legged O'Marra. Sonny went away. I went into a kitchen where Reno Starkey and four other men sat around a table that had a lot of beer on it. I noticed that two automatic pistols hung on nails over the top of the door through which I had come. They would be handy if any of the house's occupants opened the door, found an enemy with a gun there, and were told to put up their hands.

Reno poured me a glass of beer and led me through the dining room into a front room. A man lay on his belly there, with one eye to the crack between the drawn blind and the bottom of the window, watching the street.

'Go back and get yourself some beer,' Reno told him.

He got up and went away. We made ourselves comfortable in adjoining chairs.

'When I fixed up that Tanner alibi for you,' Reno said, 'I told you I was doing it because I needed all the friends I could get.'

'You got one.'

'Crack the alibi yet?' he asked.

'Not yet.'

'It'll hold,' he assured me, 'unless they got too damned much on you. Think they have?'

I did think so. I said:

'No. McGraw's just feeling playful. That'll take care of itself. How's your end holding up?'

He emptied his glass, wiped his mouth on the back of a hand, and said:

'I'll make out. But that's what I wanted to see you about. Here's how she stacks up. Pete's throwed in with McGraw. That lines coppers and beer mob up against me and Whisper. But hell! Me and Whisper are busier trying to put the chive in each other than bucking the combine. That's a sour racket. While we're tangling, them bums will eat us up.'

I said I had been thinking the same thing. He went on:

'Whisper'll listen to you. Find him, will you? Put it to him. Here's the proposish: he means to get me for knocking off Jerry Hooper, and I mean to get him first. Let's forget that for a couple of days. Nobody won't have to trust nobody else. Whisper don't ever show in any of his jobs anyways. He just sends the boys. I'll do the same this time. We'll just put the mobs together to swing the caper. We run them together, rub out the damned Finn, and then we'll have plenty of time to go gunning among ourselves.

'Put it to him cold. I don't want him to get any ideas that I'm dodging a rumpus with him or any other guy. Tell him I say if we put Pete out of the way we'll have more room to do our own scrapping in. Pete's holed-up down in Whiskeytown. I ain't got enough men to go down there and pull him out. Neither has Whisper. The two of us together has. Put it to him.'

'Whisper,' I said, 'is dead.'

Reno said, 'Is that so?' as if he thought it wasn't.

'Dan Rolff killed him yesterday morning, down in the old Redman warehouse, stuck him with the ice pick Whisper had used on the girl.'

Reno asked:

'You know this? You're not just running off at the head?'

'I know it.'

'Damned funny none of his mob act like he was gone,' he said, but he was beginning to believe me.

'They don't know it. He was hiding out, with Ted Wright the only one in on the where. Ted knew it. He cashed in on it.

He told me he got a hundred or a hundred and fifty from you, through Peak Murry.'

'I'd have given the big umpchay twice that for the straight dope,' Reno grumbled. He rubbed his chin and said: 'Well, that settles the Whisper end.'

I said: 'No.'

'What do you mean, no?'

'If his mob don't know where he is,' I suggested, 'let's tell them. They blasted him out of the can when Noonan copped him. Think they'd try it again if the news got around that McGraw had picked him up on the quiet?'

'Keep talking,' Reno said.

'If his friends try to crack the hoosegow again, thinking he's in it, that'll give the department, including Pete's specials, something to do. While they're doing it, you could try your luck in Whiskeytown.'

'Maybe,' he said slowly, 'maybe we'll try just that thing.'

'It ought to work,' I encouraged him, standing up. 'I'll see you—'

'Stick around. This is as good a spot as any while there's a reader out for you. And we'll need a good guy like you on the party.'

I didn't like that so much. I knew enough to say so. I sat down again.

Reno got busy arranging the rumor. The telephone was worked overtime. The kitchen door was worked as hard, letting men in and out. More came in than went out. The house filled with men, smoke, tension.

At half-past one Reno turned from answering a phone call to say:

'Let's take a ride.'

He went upstairs. When he came down he carried a black valise. Most of the men had gone out the kitchen door by then.

Reno gave me the black valise, saying:

'Don't wrastle it around too much.'

It was heavy.

The seven of us left in the house went out the front door and got into a curtained touring car that O'Marra had just driven up to the curb. Reno sat beside O'Marra. I was squeezed in between men in the back seat, with the valise squeezed between my legs.

Another car came out of the first cross street to run ahead of us. A third followed us. Our speed hung around forty, fast enough to get us somewhere, not fast enough to get us a lot of attention.

We had nearly finished the trip before we were bothered.

The action started in a block of one-story houses of the shack type, down in the southern end of the city.

A man put his head out of a door, put his fingers in his mouth, and whistled shrilly.

Somebody in the car behind us shot him down.

At the next corner we ran through a volley of pistol bullets.

Reno turned around to tell me:

'If they pop the bag, we'll all of us hit the moon. Get it open. We got to work fast when we get there.'

I had the fasteners unsnapped by the time we came to rest at the curb in front of a dark three-story brick building.

Men crawled all over me, opening the valise, helping themselves to the contents, bombs made of short sections of two-inch pipe, packed in sawdust in the bag. Bullets bit chunks out of the car's curtains.

Reno reached back for one of the bombs, hopped out to the sidewalk, paid no attention to a streak of blood that suddenly appeared in the middle of his left cheek, and heaved his piece of stuffed pipe at the brick building's door.

A sheet of flame was followed by deafening noise. Hunks of things pelted us while we tried to keep from being knocked over by the concussion. Then there was no door to keep anybody out of the red brick building.

A man ran forward, swung his arm, let a pipeful of hell go through the doorway. The shutters came off the downstairs windows, fire and glass flying behind them.

The car that had followed us was stationary up the street, trading shots with the neighborhood. The car that had gone ahead of us had turned into a side street. Pistol shots from behind the red brick building, between the explosions of our cargo, told us that our advance car was covering the back door.

O'Marra, out in the middle of the street, bent far over, tossed a bomb to the brick building's roof. It didn't explode. O'Marra put one foot high in the air, clawed at his throat, and fell solidly backward.

Another of our party went down under the slugs that were cutting at us from a wooden building next to the brick one.

Reno cursed stolidly and said:

'Burn them out, Fat.'

Fat spit on a bomb, ran around the back of our car, and swung his arm.

We picked ourselves up off the sidewalk, dodged flying things, and saw that the frame house was all out of whack, with flames climbing its torn edges.

'Any left?' Reno asked as we looked around, enjoying the novelty of not being shot at.

'Here's the last one,' Fat said, holding out a bomb.

Fire was dancing inside the upper windows of the brick house. Reno looked at it, took the bomb from Fat, and said:

'Back off. They'll be coming out.'

We moved away from the front of the house.

A voice indoors yelled:

'Reno!'

Reno slipped into the shadow of our car before he called back:

'Well?'

'We're done,' a heavy voice shouted. 'We're coming out. Don't shoot.'

Reno asked, 'Who's we're?'

'This is Pete,' the heavy voice said. 'There's four left of us.'

'You come first,' Reno ordered, 'with your mitts on the top of your head. The others come out one at a time, same way, after you. And half a minute apart is close enough. Come on.'

We waited a moment, and then Pete the Finn appeared in the dynamited doorway, his hands holding the top of his bald head. In the glare from the burning next-door house we could see that his face was cut, his clothes almost all torn off.

Stepping over wreckage, the bootlegger came slowly down the steps to the sidewalk.

Reno called him a lousy fish-eater and shot him four times in face and body.

Pete went down. A man behind me laughed.

Reno hurled the remaining bomb through the doorway.

We scrambled into our car. Reno took the wheel. The engine was dead. Bullets had got to it.

Reno worked the horn while the rest of us piled out.

The machine that had stopped at the corner came for us. Waiting for it, I looked up and down the street that was bright with the glow of two burning buildings. There were a few faces at windows, but whoever besides us was in the street had taken to cover. Not far away, firebells sounded.

The other machine slowed up for us to climb aboard. It was already full. We packed it in layers, with the overflow hanging on the running boards.

We bumped over dead Hank O'Marra's legs and headed for home. We covered one block of the distance with safety if not comfort. After that we had neither.

A limousine turned into the street ahead of us, came half a block toward us, put its side to us, and stopped. Out of the side, gun-fire.

Another car came around the limousine and charged us. Out of it, gun-fire.

We did our best, but we were too damned amalgamated for good fighting. You can't shoot straight holding a man in your lap, another hanging on your shoulder, while a third does his shooting from an inch behind your ear.

Our other car — the one that had been around at the building's rear — came up and gave us a hand. But by then two more had joined the opposition. Apparently Thaler's mob's attack on the jail was over, one way or the other, and Pete's army, sent to help there, had returned in time to spoil our get-away. It was a sweet mess.

I leaned over a burning gun and yelled in Reno's ear:

'This is the bunk. Let's us extras get out and do our wrangling from the street.'

He thought that a good idea, and gave orders:

'Pile out some of you hombres, and take them from the pavements.'

I was the first man out, with my eye on a dark alley entrance.

Fat followed me to it. In my shelter, I turned on him and growled:

'Don't pile up on me. Pick your own hole. There's a cellarway that looks good.'

He agreeably trotted off toward it, and was shot down at his third step.

I explored my alley. It was only twenty feet long, and ended against a high board fence with a locked gate.

A garbage can helped me over the gate into a brick-paved yard. The side fence of that yard let me into another, and from that I got into another, where a fox terrier raised hell at me.

I kicked the pooch out of the way, made the opposite fence, untangled myself from a clothes line, crossed two more yards, got yelled at from a window, had a bottle thrown at me, and dropped into a cobblestoned back street.

The shooting was behind me, but not far enough. I did all I could to remedy that. I must have walked as many streets as I did in my dreams the night Dinah was killed.

My watch said it was three-thirty a.m. when I looked at it on Elihu Willsson's front steps.

# 26
# Blackmail

had to push my client's doorbell a lot before I got any play on
it.

Finally the door was opened by the tall sunburned chauffeur. He was dressed in undershirt and pants, and had a billiard
cue in one fist.

'What do you want?' he demanded, and then, when he got
another look at me: 'It's you, is it? Well, what do you want?'

'I want to see Mr Willsson.'

'At four in the morning? Go on with you,' and he started to
close the door.

I put a foot against it. He looked from my foot to my face,
hefted the billiard cue, and asked:

'You after getting your kneecap cracked?'

'I'm not playing,' I insisted. 'I've got to see the old man. Tell
him.'

'I don't have to tell him. He told me no later than this
afternoon that if you come around he didn't want to see you.'

'Yeah?' I took the four love letters out of my pocket, picked
out the first and least idiotic of them, held it out to the chauffeur, and said: 'Give him that and tell him I'm sitting on the
steps with the rest of them. Tell him I'll sit here five minutes

and then carry the rest of them to Tommy Robins of the Consolidated Press.'

The chauffeur scowled at the letter, said, 'To hell with Tommy Robins and his blind aunt!' took the letter, and closed the door.

Four minutes later he opened the door again and said:

'Inside you.'

I followed him upstairs to old Elihu's bedroom.

My client sat up in bed with his love letter crushed in one round pink fist, its envelope in the other.

His short white hair bristled. His round eyes were as much red as blue. The parallel lines of his mouth and chin almost touched. He was in a lovely humor.

As soon as he saw me he shouted:

'So after all your brave talking you had to come back to the old pirate to have your neck saved, did you?'

I said I didn't anything of the sort. I said if he was going to talk like a sap he ought to lower his voice so that people in Los Angeles wouldn't learn what a sap he was.

The old boy let his voice out another notch, bellowing:

'Because you've stolen a letter or two that don't belong to you, you needn't think you—'

I put fingers in my ears. They didn't shut out the noise, but they insulted him into cutting the bellowing short.

I took the fingers out and said:

'Send the flunkey away so we can talk. You won't need him. I'm not going to hurt you.'

He said, 'Get out,' to the chauffeur.

The chauffeur, looking at me without fondness, left us, closing the door.

Old Elihu gave me the rush act, demanding that I surrender the rest of the letters immediately, wanting to know loudly and profanely where I had got them, what I was doing with them, threatening me with this, that, and the other, but mostly just cursing me.

I didn't surrender the letters. I said:

'I took them from the man you hired to recover them. A tough break for you that he had to kill the girl.'

Enough red went out of the old man's face to leave it normally pink. He worked his lips over his teeth, screwed up his eyes at me, and said:

'Is that the way you're going to play it?'

His voice came comparatively quiet from his chest. He had settled down to fight.

I pulled a chair over beside the bed, sat down, put as much amusement as I could in a grin, and said:

'That's one way.'

He watched me, working his lips, saying nothing. I said:

'You're the damndest client I ever had. What do you do? You hire me to clean town, change your mind, run out on me, work against me until I begin to look like a winner, then get on the fence, and now when you think I'm licked again, you don't even want to let me in the house. Lucky for me I happened to run across those letters.'

He said: 'Blackmail.'

I laughed and said:

'Listen who's naming it. All right, call it that.' I tapped the edge of the bed with a forefinger. 'I'm not licked, old top. I've won. You came crying to me that some naughty men had taken your little city away from you. Pete the Finn, Lew Yard, Whisper Thaler, and Noonan. Where are they now?

'Yard died Tuesday morning, Noonan the same night, Whisper Wednesday morning, and the Finn a little while ago. I'm giving your city back to you whether you want it or not. If that's blackmail, O.K. Now here's what you're going to do. You're going to get hold of your mayor, I suppose the lousy village has got one, and you and he are going to phone the governor— Keep still until I get through.

'You're going to tell the governor that your city police have got out of hand, what with bootleggers sworn in as officers, and so on. You're going to ask him for help – the national guard would be best. I don't know how various ruckuses around town have come out, but I do know the big boys – the ones you were afraid of – are dead. The ones that had too much on you for you to stand up to them. There are plenty of busy young men working like hell right now, trying to get into the dead men's shoes. The more, the better. They'll make it easier for the white-collar soldiers to take hold while everything is disorganized. And none of the substitutes are likely to have enough on you to do much damage.

'You're going to have the mayor, or the governor, whichever it comes under, suspend the whole Personville police department, and let the mail-order troops handle things till you can organize another. I'm told that the mayor and the governor are both pieces of your property. They'll do what you tell them. And that's what you're going to tell them. It can be done, and it's got to be done.

'Then you'll have your city back, all nice and clean and ready to go to the dogs again. If you don't do it, I'm going to turn these love letters of yours over to the newspaper buzzards, and I don't mean your *Herald* crew – the press associations. I got the letters from Dawn. You'll have a lot of fun proving that you didn't hire him to recover them, and that he didn't kill the girl doing it. But the fun you'll have is nothing to the fun people will have reading these letters. They're hot. I haven't laughed so much over anything since the hogs ate my kid brother.'

I stopped talking.

The old man was shaking, but there was no fear in his shaking. His face was purple again. He opened his mouth and roared:

'Publish them and be damned!'

I took them out of my pocket, dropped them on his bed, got up from my chair, put on my hat, and said:

'I'd give my right leg to be able to believe that the girl was killed by somebody you sent to get the letters. By God, I'd like to top off the job by sending you to the gallows!'

He didn't touch the letters. He said:

'You told me the truth about Thaler and Pete?'

'Yeah. But what difference does it make? You'll only be pushed around by somebody else.'

He threw the bedclothes aside and swung his stocky pajamaed legs and pink feet over the edge of the bed.

'Have you got the guts,' he barked, 'to take the job I offered you once before – chief of police?'

'No. I lost my guts out fighting your fights while you were hiding in bed and thinking up new ways of disowning me. Find another wet nurse.'

He glared at me. Then shrewd wrinkles came around his eyes.

He nodded his old head and said:

'You're afraid to take the job. So you did kill the girl?'

I left him as I had left him the last time, saying, 'Go to hell!' and walking out.

The chauffeur, still toting his billiard cue, still regarding me without fondness, met me on the ground floor and took me to the door, looking as if he hoped I would start something. I didn't. He slammed the door after me.

The street was gray with the beginning of daylight.

Up the street a black coupé stood under some trees. I couldn't see if anyone was in it. I played safe by walking in the opposite direction. The coupé moved after me.

There is nothing in running down streets with automobiles in pursuit. I stopped, facing this one. It came on. I took my hand away from my side when I saw Mickey Linehan's red face through the windshield.

He swung the door open for me to get in.

'I thought you might come up here,' he said as I sat beside him, 'but I was a second or two too late. I saw you go in, but was too far away to catch you.'

'How'd you make out with the police?' I asked. 'Better keep driving while we talk.'

'I didn't know anything, couldn't guess anything, didn't have any idea of what you were working on, just happened to hit town and meet you. Old friends – that line. They were still trying when the riot broke. They had me in one of the little offices across from the assembly room. When the circus cut loose I back-windowed them.'

'How'd the circus wind up?' I asked.

'The coppers shot hell out of them. They got the tip-off half an hour ahead of time, and had the whole neighborhood packed with specials. Seems it was a juicy row while it lasted – no duck soup for the coppers at that. Whisper's mob, I hear.'

'Yeah. Reno and Pete the Finn tangled tonight. Hear anything about it?'

'Only that they'd had it.'

'Reno killed Pete and ran into an ambush on the getaway. I don't know what happened after that. Seen Dick?'

'I went up to his hotel and was told he'd checked out to catch the evening train.'

'I sent him back home,' I explained. 'He seemed to think I'd killed Dinah Brand. He was getting on my nerves with it.'

'Well?'

'You mean, did I kill her? I don't know, Mickey. I'm trying to find out. Want to keep riding with me, or want to follow Dick back to the Coast?'

Mickey said:

'Don't get so cocky over one lousy murder that maybe didn't happen. But what the hell? You know you didn't lift her dough and pretties.'

'Neither did the killer. They were still there after eight that morning, when I left. Dan Rolff was in and out between then and nine. He wouldn't have taken them. The – I've got it! The coppers that found the body – Shepp and Vanaman – got there at nine-thirty. Besides the jewelry and money, some letters old Willsson had written the girl were – must have been – taken. I found them later in Dawn's pocket. The two dicks disappeared just about then. See it?

'When Shepp and Vanaman found the girl dead they looted the joint before they turned in the alarm. Old Willsson being a millionaire, his letters looked good to them, so they took them along with the other valuables, and turned them – the letters – over to the shyster to peddle back to Elihu. But Dawn was killed before he could do anything on that end. I took the letters. Shepp and Vanaman, whether they did or didn't know that the letters were not found in the dead man's possession, got cold feet. They were afraid the letters would be traced to them. They had the money and jewelry. They lit out.'

'Sounds fair enough,' Mickey agreed, 'but it don't seem to put any fingers on any murderers.'

'It clears the way some. We'll try to clear it some more. See if you can find Porter Street and an old warehouse called Redman. The way I got it, Rolff killed Whisper there, walked up to him and stabbed him with the ice pick he had found in the girl. If he did it that way, then Whisper hadn't killed her. Or he would have been expecting something of the sort, and wouldn't have let the lunger get that close to him. I'd like to look at their remains and check up.'

'Porter's over beyond King,' Mickey said. 'We'll try the south end first. It's nearer and more likely to have warehouses. Where do you set this Rolff guy?'

'Out. If he killed Whisper for killing the girl, that marks him off. Besides, she had bruises on her wrist and cheek, and he wasn't strong enough to rough her. My notion is that he left the hospital, spent the night God knows where, showed up at the girl's house after I left that morning, let himself in with his key, found her, decided Whisper had done the trick, took the sticker out of her, and went hunting Whisper.'

'So?' Mickey said. 'Now where do you get the idea that you might be the boy who put it over.'

'Stop it,' I said grouchily as we turned into Porter Street. 'Let's find our warehouse.'

# 27
# Warehouses

We rode down the street, jerking our eyes around, hunting for buildings that looked like deserted warehouses. It was light enough by now to see well.

Presently I spotted a big square rusty-red building set in the center of a weedy lot. Disuse stuck out all over lot and building. It had the look of a likely candidate.

'Pull up at the next corner,' I said. 'That looks like the dump. You stick with the heap while I scout it.'

I walked two unnecessary blocks so I could come into the lot behind the building. I crossed the lot carefully, not sneaking, but not making any noise I could avoid.

I tried the back door cautiously. It was locked, of course. I moved over to a window, tried to look in, couldn't because of gloom and dirt, tried the window, and couldn't budge it.

I went to the next window with the same luck. I rounded the corner of the building and began working my way along the north side. The first window had me beaten. The second went up slowly with my push, and didn't make much noise doing it.

Across the inside of the window frame, from top to bottom, boards were nailed. They looked solid and strong from where I stood.

I cursed them, and remembered hopefully that the window hadn't made much noise when I raised it. I climbed up on the sill, put a hand against the boards, and tried them gently.

They gave.

I put more weight behind my hand. The boards went away from the left side of the frame, showing me a row of shiny nail points.

I pushed them back farther, looked past them, saw nothing but darkness, heard nothing.

With my gun in my right fist, I stepped over the sill, down into the building. Another step to the left put me out of the window's gray light.

I switched my gun to my left hand and used my right to push the boards back over the window.

A full minute of breathless listening got me nothing. Holding my gun-arm tight to my side, I began exploring the joint. Nothing but the floor came under my feet as I inch-by-inched them forward. My groping left hand felt nothing until it touched a rough wall. I seemed to have crossed a room that was empty.

I moved along the wall, hunting for a door. Half a dozen of my undersized steps brought me to one. I leaned an ear against it, and heard no sound.

I found the knob, turned it softly, eased the door back.

Something swished.

I did four things all together: let go the knob, jumped, pulled trigger, and had my left arm walloped with something hard and heavy as a tombstone.

The flare of my gun showed me nothing. It never does, though it's easy to think you've seen things. Not knowing what else to do, I fired again, and once more.

An old man's voice pleaded:

'Don't do that, partner. You don't have to do that.'

I said: 'Make a light.'

A match spluttered on the floor, kindled, and put flickering yellow light on a battered face. It was an old face of the useless, characterless sort that goes well with park benches. He was sitting on the floor, his stringy legs sprawled far apart. He didn't seem hurt anywhere. A table leg lay beside him.

'Get up and make a light,' I ordered, 'and keep matches burning until you've done it.'

He struck another match, sheltered it carefully with his hands as he got up, crossed the room, and lit a candle on a three-legged table.

I followed him, keeping close. My left arm was numb or I would have taken hold of him for safety.

'What are you doing here?' I asked when the candle was burning.

I didn't need his answer. One end of the room was filled with wooden cases piled six high, branded *Perfection Maple Syrup*.

While the old man explained that as God was his keeper he didn't know anything about it, that all he knew was that a man named Yates had two days ago hired him as night watchman, and if anything was wrong he was as innocent as innocent, I pulled part of the top off one case.

The bottles inside had Canadian Club labels that looked as if they had been printed with a rubber stamp.

I left the cases and, driving the old man in front of me with the candle, searched the building. As I expected, I found nothing to indicate that this was the warehouse Whisper had occupied.

By the time we got back to the room that held the liquor my left arm was strong enough to lift a bottle. I put it in my pocket and gave the old man some advice:

'Better clear out. You were hired to take the place of some of the men Pete the Finn turned into special coppers. But Pete's dead now and his racket has gone blooey.'

When I climbed out the window the old man was standing in front of the cases, looking at them with greedy eyes while he counted on his fingers.

*

'Well?' Mickey asked when I returned to him and his coupé.

I took out the bottle of anything but Canadian Club, pulled the cork, passed it to him, and then put a shot into my own system.

He asked, 'Well?' again.

I said: 'Let's try to find the old Redman warehouse.'

He said: 'You're going to ruin yourself some time telling people too much,' and started the car moving.

Three blocks farther up the street we saw a faded sign, *Redman & Company*. The building under the sign was long, low, and narrow, with corrugated iron roof and few windows.

'We'll leave the boat around the corner,' I said. 'And you'll go with me this time. I didn't have a whole lot of fun by myself last trip.'

When we climbed out of the coupé, an alley ahead promised a path to the warehouse's rear. We took it.

A few people were wandering through the streets, but it was still too early for the factories that filled most of this part of town to come to life.

At the rear of our building we found something interesting. The back door was closed. Its edge, and the edge of the frame, close to the lock, were scarred. Somebody had worked there with a jimmy.

Mickey tried the door. It was unlocked. Six inches at a time, with pauses between, he pushed it far enough back to let us squeeze in.

When we squeezed in we could hear a voice. We couldn't make out what the voice was saying. All we could hear was the faint rumble of a distant man's voice, with a suggestion of quarrelsomeness in it.

Mickey pointed a thumb at the door's scar and whispered.

'Not coppers.'

I took two steps inside, keeping my weight on my rubber heels. Mickey followed, breathing down the back of my neck.

Ted Wright had told me Whisper's hiding place was in the back, upstairs. The distant rumbling voice could have been coming from there.

I twisted my face around to Mickey and said:

'Flashlight?'

He put it in my left hand. I had my gun in my right. We crept forward.

The door, still a foot open, let in enough light to show us the way across this room to a doorless doorway. The other side of the doorway was black.

I flicked the light across the blackness, found a door, shut off the light, and went forward. The next squirt of light showed us steps leading up.

We went up the steps as if we were afraid they would break under our feet.

The rumbling voice had stopped. There was something else in the air. I didn't know what. Maybe a voice not quite loud enough to be heard, if that meant anything.

I had counted nine steps when a voice spoke clearly above us. It said:

'Sure, I killed the bitch.'

A gun said something, the same thing four times, roaring like a 16-inch rifle under the iron roof.

The first voice said: 'All right.'

By that time Mickey and I had put the rest of the steps behind us, had shoved a door out of the way, and were trying to pull Reno Starkey's hands away from Whisper's throat.

It was a tough job and a useless one. Whisper was dead.

Reno recognized me and let his hands go limp.

His eyes were as dull, his horse face as wooden, as ever.

Mickey carried the dead gambler to the cot that stood in one end of the room, spreading him on it.

The room, apparently once an office, had two windows. In their light I could see a body stowed under the cot – Dan Rolff. A Colt's service automatic lay in the middle of the floor.

Reno bent his shoulders, swaying.

'Hurt?' I asked.

'He put all four in me,' he said, calmly, bending to press both forearms against his lower body.

'Get a doc,' I told Mickey.

'No good,' Reno said. 'I got no more belly left than Peter Collins.'

I pulled a folding chair over and sat him down on it, so he could lean forward and hold himself together.

Mickey ran out and down the stairs.

'Did you know he wasn't croaked?' Reno asked.

'No. I gave it to you the way I got it from Ted Wright.'

'Ted left too soon,' he said. 'I was leary of something like that, and came to make sure. He trapped me pretty, playing dead till I was under the gun.' He stared dully at Whisper's corpse. 'Game at that, damn him. Dead, but wouldn't lay down, bandaging hisself, laying here waiting by hisself.' He smiled, the only smile I had ever seen him use. 'But he's just meat and not much of it now.'

His voice was thickening. A little red puddle formed under the edge of his chair. I was afraid to touch him. Only the pressure of his arms, and his bent-forward position, were keeping him from falling apart.

He stared at the puddle and asked:

'How the hell did you figure you didn't croak her?'

'I had to take it out in hoping I hadn't, till just now,' I said. 'I had you pegged for it, but couldn't be sure. I was all hopped up that night, and had a lot of dreams, with bells ringing and voices calling, and a lot of stuff like that. I got an idea maybe it wasn't straight dreaming so much as hop-head nightmares stirred up by things that were happening around me.

'When I woke up, the lights were out. I didn't think I killed her, turned off the light, and went back to take hold of the ice pick. But it could have happened other ways. You knew I was there that night. You gave me my alibi without stalling. That got me thinking. Dawn tried blackmailing me after he heard Helen Albury's story. The police, after hearing her story, tied you, Whisper, Rolff and me together. I found Dawn dead after seeing O'Marra half a block away. It looked like the shyster had tried blackmailing you. That and the police tying us together started me thinking the police had as much on the rest of you as on me. What they had on me was that Helen Albury had seen me go in or out or both that night. It was a good guess they had the same on the rest of you. There were reasons for counting Whisper and Rolff out. That left you – and me. But why you killed her's got me puzzled.'

'I bet you,' he said, watching the red puddle grow on the floor. 'It was her own damned fault. She calls me up, tells me Whisper's coming to see her, and says if I get there first I can bushwhack him. I'd like that. I go over there, stick around, but he don't show.'

He stopped, pretending interest in the shape the red puddle was taking. I knew pain had stopped him, but I knew he would go on talking as soon as he got himself in hand. He meant to die as he had lived, inside the same tough shell. Talking could be torture, but he wouldn't stop on that account, not while anybody was there to see him. He was Reno Starkey who could take anything the world had without batting an eye, and he would play it out that way to the end.

'I got tired of waiting,' he went on after a moment. 'I hit her door and asked how come. She takes me in, telling me there's nobody there. I'm doubtful, but she swears she's alone, and we go back in the kitchen. Knowing her, I'm beginning to think maybe it's me and not Whisper that's being trapped.'

Mickey came in, telling us he had phoned for an ambulance.

Reno used the interruption to rest his voice, and then continued with his story:

'Later, I find that Whisper did phone her he was coming, and got there before me. You were coked. She was afraid to let him in, so he beat it. She don't tell me that, scared I'll go and leave

213

her. You're hopped and she wants protection against Whisper coming back. I don't know none of that then. I'm leary that I've walked into something, knowing her. I think I'll take hold of her and slap the truth out of her. I try it, and she grabs the pick and screams. When she squawks, I hear a man's feet hitting the floor. The trap's sprung, I think.'

He spoke slower, taking more time and pains to turn each word out calmly and deliberately, as talking became harder. His voice had become blurred, but if he knew it he pretended he didn't.

'I don't mean to be the only one that's hurt. I twist the pick out of her hand and stick it in her. You gallop out, coked to the edges, charging at the whole world with both eyes shut. She tumbles into you. You go down, roll around till your hand hits the butt of the pick. Holding on to that, you go to sleep, peaceful as she is. I see it then, what I've done. But hell! she's croaked. There's nothing to do about it. I turn off the lights and go home. When you—'

A tired looking ambulance crew – Poisonville gave them plenty of work – brought a litter into the room, ending Reno's tale. I was glad of it. I had all the information I wanted, and sitting there listening to and watching him talk himself to death wasn't pleasant.

I took Mickey over to a corner of the room and muttered in his ear:

'The job's yours from now on. I'm going to duck. I ought to be in the clear, but I know my Poisonville too well to take any chances. I'll drive your car to some way station where I can catch a train for Ogden. I'll be at the Roosevelt Hotel there, registered as P. F. King. Stay with the job, and let me know when it's wise to either take my own name again or a trip to Honduras.'

I spent most of my week in Ogden trying to fix up my reports so they would not read as if I had broken as many Agency rules, state laws and human bones as I had.

Mickey arrived on the sixth night.

He told me that Reno was dead, that I was no longer officially a criminal, that most of the First National Bank stick-up loot had been recovered, that MacSwain had confessed killing Tim Noonan, and that Personville, under martial law, was developing into a sweet-smelling thornless bed of roses.

Mickey and I went back to San Francisco.

I might just as well have saved the labor and sweat I had put into trying to make my reports harmless. They didn't fool the Old Man. He gave me merry hell.